I0571095

The Mage and The Boffin

Part 1 – The Early Stories

by Cliff Pratt

ISBN : 978-0-473-46190-4

Licence Notes

By this Author

The Last Beautiful Woman (available in digital and paperback formats)

How I Wrote and Self Published My First Book (available in digital format)

The Mage and The Boffin (available in digital format)

The Mage and The Boffin Part 1 & 2 (available in paperback, late 2018)

Author and Publisher Details

Published by Cliff Pratt
Author : Cliff Pratt
Email : enkidu@cliffp.com
Or : enkiduonthenet@gmail.com
Website : https://www.cliffp.com

Table of Contents

Introducing the Mage and the Boffin

"How would you introduce yourself to a reader, my dear?" asked the Mage.

"Mmm, you mean someone has written about us?" said the Boffin.

"You know they have. Many people have over the years. They've called us by different names, it's true."

"Well, I'm a scientist, hence 'the Boffin', and my powers are the powers of Science. It's obvious isn't it?"

"What about me?"

"Your field is magic, hence 'the Mage' Your powers are based in Magic."

"Yes. Always the obvious answer! Is that all?"

"What do you mean? I'm a scientist and you're a magician. That's true, isn't it?"

"What about logic, philosophy, feelings, thoughts, mathematics, mind, biology, babies, medicine, dragons, kings and queens, politics."

"Oh I see. Well, there is a blurry area, I suppose. But I started out as a physicist, of course. Pure science. Measurements and observations. Theories and hypotheses. Before we got our powers."

"And now? After all the years that you've known me? Has that changed your view of yourself and the world? What about me and our kids? Do you measure and observe us?"

"The truth? Well, I wouldn't be me if I didn't measure and observe! But it doesn't stop me from loving you all."

"Would it surprise you that I also measure and observe you and our kids?

"No, it wouldn't surprise me. But you aren't so interested in theories as I am. You're more interested in connections, relationships, the mind and consciousness, and that sort of stuff. You measure things in a different way. We are both highly logical people, but I thought that you weren't when we met. That was just plain prejudice, though, because we were on opposite sides in a war! So, to answer your earlier question, yes, knowing you has changed my view of myself and others."

"There's not much difference between our fields, then?" he said teasingly.

She smiled and took him seriously, as he knew she would, and considered.

"Well," she said, "not as much as one might think. But I'm interested in analysis, you're interested in synthesis. I'm interested in objects, you're interested in feelings. I talk in terms of neurones, and you talk about motives and intentions. We have much the same interests, but we look at things differently. I'm generalising, of course."

"It's interesting that I am the one asking the questions and you are the one answering them," he said.

Once again, she took him seriously.

"Yes," she nodded. "That is a good indication of how we work together. You spot the problems, and suggest solutions. Then I implement them."

"Don't you mean that you go rushing in there headlong?"

She sniffed and said "You might think that, and you might not be totally wrong."

She tried not laugh, but couldn't help it.

"But you yourself don't hold back, and we always present a united front," she added.

He nodded his agreement.

"What sort of stories should be written about us, dear?" she asked.

"And our family and friends. They'll be there too."

"Yes, true. We will only be bit players in some of the tales."

"'What sort of stories'? We go back a long time, so the older stories will seem strange to people these days, if they are told exactly as they happened. People trapped by spells in trees and so on. So stories from the earlier times might best be written like folk-tales or fairy stories. But the stories from more modern times can be written in a more modern style. It doesn't make a lot of difference, though, so long as they tell the stories properly."

"Should the stories explain the science and the magic, do you think?" she asked.

"Only when necessary. The science doesn't much differ from the modern science in practical ways. It depends a lot on measurements and physical devices. The magic will just confuse people, these days, because they aren't used to thinking in magical terms, and because of that, it won't make sense to them. And if the author tried to explain how our powers are related to the fields which we represent, the author would need to write a whole extra book."

"True. We've only worked out about sixty to seventy per sent of how our powers work ourselves. That reminds me. We should write down what we know for our successors, but it isn't really part of our stories, is it?"

"Good idea. But what about us personally? Our looks?"

"Well, you're a tall, handsome man. You wear ordinary slacks and shirts most times these days, but sometimes you wear the full regalia, the long robes, and carry a rod or wand.

You rarely wear a hat but sometimes have a hood. You have long sensitive fingers and have a full beard and tend to wear your hair longish. Your skin is light brown, a bit lighter than mine, and your eyes are deep, deep brown. And I love you dearly. What about me?"

"You are the glow of a sunrise, the tinkle of water in a stream, and the warmth of a fire in winter, and I love you dearly."

She gave him a look, and he sighed.

"OK, OK! For the record! You are a beautiful brown skinned woman, quite slender, with long brown hair (usually!). You generally wear shirts and slacks like me. On rare occasions, you wear a dress and scrub up quite well!"

"Hey!" she interjected.

"Sometimes you wear a white coat and I've known you wear eye glasses for effect. You are marvellous with kids, especially babies, and at one time we were barely ever without one around. Ours, or someone else's. In spite of your calling you are emotional and caring, and more than a little impetuous. However, if you are deep in the throes of an experiment or serious study, you can be extremely uncommunicative and distracted, to the point of being antisocial."

"Wow! What about us as a couple?" she asked.

"We definitely complement each and together we are stronger than either of us alone. We share a lot of traits in common. You called me a synthesist but I can be analytical, like now. I'm the one who is supposed to be emotionally driven and impulsive, but you excel in those areas! You're not afraid to use magic, and I use science when it is appropriate. You worried at one time that we were becoming too alike. Or was that me? Neither of us want to rule the world, but both of us like to be in control of the situation."

"What about our 'powers'?"

"We get our powers as a consequence of our roles. Yours are based on your role as focus of Science, and usually, but not always, you use a 'device' of some sort. I am the focus of Magic, and I don't usually use a device, but frequently use gestures and signs. Sometimes the effects of our different powers are pretty much the same. We try to use our powers as little as possible, because as often as not complications arise."

"Mmmm. Are we nice people?"

She stroked his beard and he kissed her.

"I think that people would say we are," he said. "Of course, we are forceful at times. The roles require it now and then. But we are sociable people and I like our friends and I think that they like us."

She nodded and sighed. He put his arm round her, and she leant against him. She curled her legs up on the sofa, and the two of them stayed there like that for some time. She opened and read a journal, while the Mage studied patterns in a scrying ball. Two of the most powerful people in many worlds, (or, as they would say 'spaces'), just relaxing at home.

***

The King Gets What He Wants

There once was a land divided. Each small Kingdom fought against all the other small Kingdoms, and as is usual in such cases, the people suffered. They died as armies fought over their towns and starved as armies criss-crossed their fields and destroyed their crops. Their children died as the Kings and Queens enlisted them into their armies by force.

The Mage and the Boffin watched this from their safe space. Their three sons watched as well, and were horrified.

"Please do something, Dad. Make them stop, Mum," their eldest begged.

"Yes, we need to do something, my dear." said the Mage. "But what?"

"I know," said his wife, the Boffin. "We'll make a safe space, like this one, and we'll invite all the Kings and Queens there, and when they are there, this is what we'll do...."

So the Mage created a new safe space, big enough to contain all the Kings and Queens and the Boffin made houses for them to live in, and the Boffin built a large building for the Kings and Queens to gather in. But none of the Kings or Queens would come.

The Boffin sighed. "You'll have to fetch them, dear."

So the Mage did. All over the land, the Kings and the Queens disappeared and reappeared in the safe space, and all the wars petered out.

The Mage and the Boffin appeared in front of the Kings and Queens and said "You are our guests for as long as it takes for you to make peace."

"Peace? I'll give you peace," said one King.

He drew his sword and charged the Mage and the Boffin and brought it down on the Mage's head, but the sword passed through him as if he was made of air.

The Mage sighed. "I'm not actually here. What you see is a hologram created by the Boffin. And I have just cast a spell on this space, so that weapons cannot be used. If you try to use a weapon, it will burn you."

The King's sword became red-hot, and he dropped it.

"We'll not be forced to make peace by you! We'll break out and raise armies and kill you!" he raged.

It took a year and a day. At first the Kings and Queens fought each other, wrestling and punching, since they couldn't use weapons, but this was undignified and didn't solve anything. They tried to escape, building ladders and digging tunnels, but they couldn't get out of the safe space. So they started talking to one another, started forming groups and alliances, and eventually, they came together in one big Parliament and made peace.

The Kings and Queens rejoiced and the Mage and the Boffin commended them. They sent the Kings and the Queens back to their homes, and the people rejoiced. Everyone laid down their weapons.

However, one King had a sliver of hatred in his heart hidden so well that the Boffin could not detect it with her instruments, and the Mage could not see it with his charms and spells. The King's armies cruelly ravaged all the Kingdoms and welded all the Kingdoms into one nation which the King ruled by force, savagely.

"That wasn't supposed to happen," said the Mage to the Boffin.

"We will have to do something about it," said the Boffin, but before they could decide what to do, the King summoned them.

"I have your sons," he said, gesturing.

A screen was drawn aside and their three sons stood there in chains.

The Boffin gave him a look which chilled him to the core. "You had better not harm a hair of their heads, or you will have me to reckon with. AND TAKE THOSE CHAINS OFF!"

The King gestured and the chains were removed.

The King said "You will now perform three tasks for me, and I will release one of your sons as each task is completed. Your first task is to build me a castle, one that surpasses all other castles in the country. It must be impregnable."

The Mage and the Boffin worked away together for a month and a day, and produced an oval object the size of a football.

When they presented it to the King, he said, "What is this?"

The Boffin said "It's the egg of your castle. Put it where you want the castle to be, tap it gently three times and it will grow into the castle. It will take a year and a day to complete."

The King was pleased and took the egg to the top of a ridge which ran down the side of a mountain close by. He carefully placed the egg and rapped it three times. The egg flowed outwards and formed a platform, the platform extended sideways, and walls started to grow out of the platform. Everything was a brilliant white to start with, but hints of colour started to appear. The material of the Castle merged into the rocks of the mountain. A darker rectangular area on a wall grew protrusions, and turned into a door. The King stepped up to it and pulled it open. He laughed with joy.

"You can have your youngest son back in a year and a day," said the King.

The Mage and the Boffin looked at each.

"Don't worry," called the eldest son. "We'll be OK."

"It might do them some good," said the Boffin, "They will be safe."

So they let the King keep the boys.

After a year and a day the Mage and the Boffin were called to the King's presence. The three sons were standing by his side.

"I release your youngest son, as agreed," said the King.

"We agreed to nothing," said the Boffin coldly, and the King wisely decided not to comment.

The youngest son walked over to his mother and father.

"Are you OK, my son?" asked the Mage.

The boy nodded. "We're OK. We mostly lived with the King's son and his daughter. His son is nice, and made us as welcome as he could. His daughter is OK for a girl, too."

The Mage and the Boffin smiled.

"The next thing that I want, is to be able to fly from one end of the Kingdom to the other. When I can do that, you can have your middle son back."

The Mage looked at the Boffin. "Can you handle this one, my dear?"

"Yes, of course. It will take me three months and a day."

So the Boffin retreated to her workshop. Crashing and banging could be heard, and the sounds of drills and saws. The bright flashing light of welding torches leaked from the cracks around doorways and the shuttered windows. After three months and a day she rolled a machine out of her workshop. It had an engine at the front to pull it through the air and great solid wings to hold it up in the sky.

"Here are the plans for the machine," she said handing them to the King. "I've trained one of your pages to fly it, and it will go from one end of your Kingdom to the other in about a day. Now give me back my son."

"Not so fast," said the King.

He jumped in the machine with the page and the page flew the machine round and round the Palace, then back to where the Mage and the Boffin were waiting.

"I suppose you fulfilled my request," he said grudgingly. "I release your middle son."

And the middle son was allowed to join his parents and his younger brother.

"How are you, my love?" his mother asked.

He nodded. "Pretty good. The King's son was kind to us and helped us with our homework. His sister is quite nice too. We played together a lot. She's good at chess and badminton."

The King was not happy. "I wanted to fly like a bird. I didn't want a machine. So my last request, for your oldest son, is for you to make me able to fly like a bird."

"Hmm, are you sure?" asked the Mage.

"Of course I'm sure," raged the King. "Just do it."

The Mage went away and toiled for a month and a day. Pungent smells and clouds of multi-coloured smoke rolled from his laboratory. Bubbling and hissings could be heard, and he sent out for some quicksilver and the venom of a cobra. Once more he and his family stood before the King.

"In this syringe I have a medicine which will allow you to fly like a bird, with wings. Are you sure that you want me to inject you with it?"

The King bared his arm and said "Inject away."

"This will take a while to work," said the Mage, as he injected the King.

"How long," said the King suspiciously.

"A few months."

"'A few months'! Well you don't get your son back until it works!" ranted the King.

The Boffin looked at the Mage.

"Give it a week," he reassured her.

Sure enough, a week later the King called the Mage and the Boffin and their two sons in front of him. Their oldest son still stood alongside the King.

"Why am I so tired? Why am I eating so much? What is happening to me?" the King complained.

"Well, the food is a fuel for the process, and the tiredness is your body preparing for the process."

"Process? What process?"

"Metamorphosis. You will go to sleep while your body transforms. You will grow claws, your jaw will lengthen and you will grow extra teeth. You will get an extra heart and bigger lungs. Your arms will become wings."

"You're turning me into a monster?" screamed the King. But he didn't have the energy to maintain his rage and fell back into his seat. "So tired. But at least I have your son!"

The Boffin waved her hand in a pattern, and suddenly her son was by her side.

"How are you, son?"

"Pretty good, Mum. The King's son looked after us. We played soccer and swam in the pool. The King's daughter is amazing. She has long dark hair and her skin is as smooth as silk and as dark as chocolate. Her eyes are brown and as deep as a pool. She's kind and generous and..."

He looked like he could go on for a long time, but his mother stopped him.

"Your Majesty, you are not changing into a monster. You are changing into a dragon, a noble creature. It's the only creature as big as a man which can fly, though it needs physics to achieve that."

"Physics?"

"Or magic. They're much the same thing. You wanted, no, you demanded the ability to fly like a bird, and that is what we have given you."

"Reverse it!"

"I'm sorry, we can't do that. It's a one way process."

"You tricked me! Guards, arrest them!"

The Boffin waved her hands in another pattern, and a shimmer surrounded her and her family.

"We will leave you now, your Majesty," said the Mage. "Don't try to stop us and don't try to find us. You won't succeed."

They turned and walked away through the Palace. No one tried to stop them but someone called to them."

They halted. It was the King's son, and his sister, the King's daughter.

"Please, what will happen to our father? I know he isn't a good man, but he is our father."

The Mage looked into the Prince's dark brown eyes, and saw the intelligence there. He saw the compassion and the love for his fellow man in there. The Mage knew that he would make a good King. He held the boy's dark hand in his pale hand and told him the truth. The Mage judged that he could handle it.

"He will eat more and more, and will become more and more tired and will eventually fall asleep for good. His body will grow a leathery skin, and he will lie there for several months, changing internally. Eventually his body will transform into that of a dragon, and when it is ready the dragon will burst out of the skin. The tiny bit of the King that is left will fly like a bird, with wings. Don't worry, it isn't a painful process," said the Mage.

"It would be best for you to leave the Palace now," said the Boffin. "If you don't, he will infect you, and you will 'pass over' as he is going to. The firstborn of all your descendants will also 'pass over' if you are infected."

The Prince looked at the Boffin and the Mage. "He is my father. I must stay around him and help him through it. I'll take him to his Castle, and he can finish his change up there."

The Boffin put her hand on his. She was darker skinned than her husband, but her hand was still pale compared to the Prince's. "You are a brave boy and a much better man than your father. Your own change will happen when you are more than sixty. You have many useful and hopefully happy years in front of you. You will need to repair the damage that your father has done, and govern wisely. I think that you can do that. You will need to search for your bride as soon as you are able, but I assure you that she is out there and you will know her when you meet her. Something will happen."

"'Something will happen'?"

She nodded and she and her family walked away. The Boffin's oldest son kept looking back, and as they were about to take the step into the safe space, he gently waved to the King's daughter, and she waved back. To the Prince and the Princess it looked as if the Mage and the Boffin and their family had disappeared between one step and the next.

"So, son, how did you find out that the Princess's skin was as smooth as silk and that her eyes were as deep as a pool?"

"Well, I, errr.... Oh, Mum!"

***

Golden Hair and the Bears

The Mage and the Boffin had a daughter whose name was originally Jean, but which became Patricia, and then changed to Helga. They weren't sure why her name wouldn't stay the same, so they gave up and nicknamed her "Golden Hair" because of her long blond hair. And the name stuck.

At the time they were not living in their "safe space" but were living in the forests of the North West where there were few people. It was just a step from their home to their "safe space" of course, if they needed it.

Golden Hair loved to be outside and loved roaming the forests. She charmed the wolves and the owls and the reindeer and the caribou and the hawks and the squirrels and all the other non-human inhabitants of the forests.

Her mother, the Boffin, worried about her at first, but made a special device into a necklace and hung it around Golden Hair's neck, and knew that she could contact her daughter any time. The Mage also cast a charm on her to keep her safe and stowed it in the necklace. The charm also made sure that Golden Hair couldn't ever lose the necklace.

Golden Hair ran for kilometre after kilometre with the caribou, or the wolves that trailed them. She cowered under the ground with the mice, and she hovered overhead with the hawks. She hid nuts with the squirrels, and she swam in the streams with the salmon, leaping the waterfalls in a flash of silver.

She understood the cruel truth of death in the forest. The hawk lived by killing the mice and rabbits, and the wolves ate only when they came across a dead reindeer or managed to kill one. When she ran with the wolves, she helped them bring down a reindeer, and when she flew with the hawks, she stooped on the mice and other small animals.

"I'm concerned that she is spending so much time in the forest," said the Boffin one day.

"Don't worry, my dear," said the Mage. "She's learning the way of the world. She can easily catch up with the formal stuff later. She's intelligent enough."

So the Boffin let her daughter spend time in the forest. She just checked with Golden Hair every so often and made her come back for a bath now and then, and only took issue with her when she didn't completely shake off the forest when she came home.

"Golden Hair, you're shedding fur everywhere. And please cut your nails. You're scratching things."

Golden Hair, who was a good girl, said "Sorry Mum", then took a shower, unplugged the drain hole, and cut her finger and toe nails. Then she went round the house with the vacuum cleaner.

"Thanks, dear," said the Boffin and trimmed the golden hair to a reasonable length and brushed it until it gleamed.

"Thanks Mum," said Golden Hair. "I love you, you know."

"Of course, dear."

Of all the animals in the forest, Golden Hair loved the bears the most. In the section of forest closest to home there lived a family of bears, a mother bear and two two-year-old cubs. Golden Hair spent hours and days with the bear family, eating bugs and worms, berries, nuts and seeds. She broke open rotten tree trunks with her strong claws to get at the grubs, and learned with the cubs to catch the salmon leaping up the rapids. She tore into the delicious pink flesh with her strong teeth and squabbled with the cubs for the mother bear's leavings.

She lived with them for so long that she learned the language of the bears, though bears don't talk a lot.

"Why is there no father bear?" she asked the mother bear one day.

The mother bear shook the water from her coat. "I hope he stays a long way away. He would kill the cubs. Do human fathers not kill their cubs?"

Golden Hair was not shocked. Bears were not humans and did things differently.

"Why would he kill the cubs?"

"There's only so much food. And they might grow big enough to kill him or drive him off."

Golden Hair nodded in the bear fashion. It made sense from the bear point of view.

As Autumn drew on, Golden Hair and the bears started to gorge themselves on whatever they could lay their claws on. When they weren't eating, they were dozing in the sun.

One morning the ground was covered with snow.

"Time to find a place to stay," said the mother bear, leading the cubs and Golden Hair higher into the mountains. They found a place under a jutting rock, and the mother bear nodded in the bear manner.

"This will do," said the mother bear, and she and the cubs and Golden Hair scraped out the uncomfortable pebbles, twigs and other debris and settled down to sleep.

In the night a heavier fall of snow had covered the rock and built up a wall around the bears and Golden Hair. The mother bear stirred and went back to sleep. The cubs and Golden Hair didn't wake.

"Dear, look at this," said the Boffin.

On her screen, Golden Hair's necklace showed the hibernating bears and Golden Hair in the den.

"Do you want me to bring her back?" asked the Mage.

"No, let her sleep. But next spring, she will have to come back and go to school. It's time."

So the bears and Golden Hair slept through the winter, cosy in their den. Golden Hair, since she wasn't a bear, was occasionally a little restless, and woke a little, but the gentle snores of her companions and the warm smelly atmosphere soon sent her off again.

The days passed, the weeks passed, the months passed, and eventually the snug little hollow started to get a little damp as the snow began to melt. The bears and Golden Hair started to stretch and wake. They crawled out of their cosy nest and started to look for food. They found some moss and grass and ate some bark off a tree. Then they happened on a rabbit which had frozen to death, and not been found by anyone else.

The mother bear knew that Golden Hair had to go home, without actually thinking about it like a human would, so she led her cubs and Golden Hair down to the lowlands and towards Golden Hair's home. In the lower altitudes the spring flush had brought out the flowers and the grass was dense and cushioned the cubs and Golden Hair as they rolled and tumbled through the meadows.

What the mother bear didn't know and wouldn't have understood was that some of the few people who lived in the area had seen Golden Hair and reported the sightings to the Baron.

"Five hundred dollars to the man who brings me the pelt of the golden bear," he declared.

It happened that a young lad of about Golden Hair's age was walking through the forest, with his gun, looking for a turkey for the pot. He was not trying very hard, to be honest, as he didn't like killing things, but he'd shoot, if he stumbled across one.

He heard a crashing through the forest and the golden bear and two other young bears tumbled onto the track, followed by the mother bear who reared up on her hind legs. The boy saw the golden bear and remembered the bounty on its pelt. He raised his gun and shot at the golden bear.

Rings of fire spread from the golden bear and radiated into the universe. The moon glowed slightly more brightly for a second, and the boy found himself looking at a blond girl of about his own age, totally naked except for a necklace, but totally unharmed.

The mother bear lumbered forward and the boy raised his gun again, but his gun was knocked aside. The mother bear dropped to all fours and nuzzled the blond girl.

"She's only checking her out," said the Boffin, tossing a coat to her daughter and getting between her and the boy. "Why did you shoot at my daughter?"

"The, the, the Baron offered five hundred dollars for her pelt," said the lad, suddenly thinking that pelt was not a good word to use in this situation.

"Did he? I'll have to have a word with him," said the Boffin.

The boy was suddenly glad that he was not the Baron. Golden Hair walked up to him, tightening her belt around her waist.

"You're cute," she said.

"Don't mind her, she's not completely back in human mode yet," sniffed the Boffin.

"What's your name?" said Golden Hair. "I'm Golden Hair."

"Jack," said the boy.

So they walked home, with the Boffin resolutely walking between Jack and Golden Hair who kept sneaking looks at each other. The Boffin was not too displeased though, as she realised that it wouldn't be too hard to persuade Golden Hair to go to school next term.

When they got home, Golden Hair took a shower then came and gave her Mum a hug.

"Mum, the mother bear, when she nuzzled me said 'It's over.' Is it over?"

"Yes, dear, I think it's over. Now, about school...."

***

There's a Dragon on the Roof

One day the Mage came in and said "My dear, there's a dragon on the roof."

"Is there?" said the Boffin.

They both went outside to look.

"What's she doing?" asked the Boffin.

"Not much. I saw her as I came up the track from town. She's not moved much at all."

The dragon scratched herself behind her ear with the tip of her folded wing. She belched loudly, flapped her wings and took off. Flapping lazily she rose into the air and disappeared with a pop. Then she suddenly reappeared and circled to land on the roof again. She shifted from leg to leg, then repeated the whole procedure, this time without the belch.

"She obviously wants something," said the Boffin. "I wonder....."

The dragon took off again and flapped her wings and circled, then disappeared with a pop again. She reappeared and landed on the roof.

"She wants us to follow her," said the Boffin. "I'm sure of it."

She turned around and drew one of her instruments from her pocket. She pressed a button and a shimmer surrounded the house, and the dragon took off with a squawk.

"Oops, sorry dragon," she said.

"That's all locked up, and I've activated your protection charm to be safe," she said to the Mage. "Let's go."

They stepped through to the dragons' safe space. Actually, reflected the Mage, it was probably their original space. Gravity was weaker here, and the light a little dimmer than nighttime back home, but not by much. Two moons moved slowly through the sky and a smaller moon raced past them at a much faster pace. Ponderous clouds moved sluggishly across the sky. Stars crawled across the sky as the planet turned slightly faster than back home.

"Hmm, nighttime. Do we travel now or wait for dawn?" wondered the Boffin.

"She seems to want us to go now."

They had stepped across onto a reasonably flat peak and the dragon was perched on a neighbouring spire of rock. She took off and flew to another peak further away, then back again. No longer mute in her home space she trumpeted, but neither of them could yet speak dragon.

"Come on then," said the Boffin and stepped over the edge of the precipice. As she fell she opened her wings and changed her fall into a sweeping glide. She caught an updraft and swooped up to land on a peak next to the dragon.

"I wish she wouldn't do that," thought the Mage as he opened his wings and flew across to perch near her.

They couldn't talk or think human thoughts easily while they had the shape of dragons, of course, but they could understand dragon. The dragon indicated something very important was happening and that they should follow her. They all took off and headed in a direction that the Mage somehow knew was roughly north, or would have known if he was thinking the human way.

Gravity was weaker here and didn't drag the mountains down as much as it did at home, so there were high cliffs and deep steep sided valleys, incredibly steep scree slopes, tall spindly spires of rock, arches worn by the wind and rocks balanced in positions which would be impossible back home.

Water still flowed downhill, of course, but it did so in a much more leisurely way than it did back home. It was as if it wore seven league boots. It produced great spumes as it tumbled slowly downhill towards the seas and great slow falling fountains when it hit submerged rocks.

The three dragons wheeled and turned through the canyons and gulleys as if they were linked together. The Mage could sense the Boffin's exhilaration as they twisted and turned. She loved this space, and the freedom of flight. In the small part of him that was human at the moment he hoped that she would not let it go to her head, as the last time that they had ventured into this space and had flown with the dragons, she had returned home with a shoulder sprain.

They flew through the night. At one point their guide dropped down to an alpine pasture and all three dragons tore great bunches of foliage from the spindly bushes and trees. The taste made the human part of him think of mint and parsley, with a hint of resin. Small bat like creatures, this space's birds, flew away squeaking as the three big reptiles ripped up their habitat, and wingless small reptiles ran like chickens from the destruction. The dragons ignored them.

As the sun rose, its pink halo rose first, then the main yellowish body of the sun followed. The ponderous clouds swelled and billowed, rain drifted down rather than fell, dampening the jungles of the lowlands, falling on the rocks of the highlands and swelling the slow falling streams. The three dragons rose over the clouds drawing energy from the sun through their photosynthetic skins. Other dragons rose through the clouds to join them and soon a vast triangle of dragons pointed roughly north like an arrowhead.

In the middle distance a range of mountains, higher than any that the dragons had yet passed over, drew closer. As the morning drew on the clouds cleared and the countryside below proved to be broad grassy plains. Herds of animals slowly roamed the pampas, drifting along some unknown migration route.

In twos and threes the accompanying dragons dropped down and picked off the odd beast. The Mage and the Boffin and their guide dragon swooped low over the herds, automatically working together to isolate a single animal. The Mage swooped down and caught it by the neck and shook it killing it instantly.

The three dragons ripped into the carcase and scavengers circled, some in the sky and some on the ground, hoping for some leavings. Both sorts showed their reptile heritage. The three dragons ate their fill and left the rest of the beast to the scavengers. As they took off, the squabbling started over their leavings.

They rose into the sky and the arrowhead reformed behind them. The vast number of dragons in the escort had made little difference to the immense numbers of the animals below.

Slowly the mountains drew closer and details could be seen. One rocky peak soared over the rest, a needle of rock impossible at home. The peak had broad shoulders, subordinate mountains which would have been giants elsewhere. The range petered out to the east, but large peaks could be seen trending west.

The flying wedge of dragons headed directly for the massive spire. As they drew closer, a relatively flat area could be seen at the base of the needle. Dragons could be seen landing and taking off in huge numbers like bees round a busy beehive. Their guide led them through the crush to the centre of the crowd, and they set down on the ledge close to the base of the needle. Dragons were coming and going from a hole at the bottom.

Their guide roared and the other dragons scattered. She led them into the hole and their dragon night vision cut in. The dragons coming out cowered out of the way as they made their into the darkness. The passage opened into a large chamber, carpeted with large tree trunks. Light filtered down from somewhere a long way above. As they mounted the pile, the trees became branches and branches became twigs.

The Mage helped the Boffin over the edge of the nest. In the centre was a huge dragon, with skin as white as snow, almost glowing in the dim light. She weaved her head from side to side but let the two humans approach.

"Well, we're here. Now what?" said the Boffin.

She wasn't talking to the dragon, but she snorted as if in reply, and moved sideways on the nest. She had six green eggs hidden beneath her body.

The Boffin moved closer and the white dragon loomed over her. She rumbled but let the Boffin approach the eggs. They were big; the smallest was higher than the Boffin's waist. They were all vibrating and rolling from side to side.

"Oh, I think she wants us to be midwives, dear," said the Boffin.

The Mage cautiously approached. He laid a hand on one of the eggs. Suddenly a blow from inside the egg pierced it, fairly close to his hand, and cracks flowed through the shell.

The Mage jumped but stayed by the egg, holding it still. The dragonlet inside hit the shell again and a whole chunk fell away. He carefully pulled on the cracks in the shell and almost half of it came free. He tossed it away behind him and the mother dragon flicked it out of the nest.

"Don't touch the skin of the chicks," he advised. "They are still as soft as silk."

The mother dragon started making a high keening noise. The Boffin was helping another chick from its shell, and as each chick was freed it made its way to the mother dragon. Each chick shed the spike on its snout soon after breaking free.

Finally, there was only one egg left. This was rolling around, but not fracturing. Their guide dragon nudged them towards it.

"This one can't get out. It will die if it can't," said the Mage.

The Boffin picked up a stick from the nest and whacked the egg which cracked all over.

"Always the physical answer," sighed the Mage, though he conceded that he couldn't think of anything better.

"Perfectly safe if done scientifically," said the Boffin.

The Mage joined her in pulling the egg apart. They exposed the dragonlet in the egg. Except, it wasn't a dragonlet, it was a human baby.

"Oh my," said the Boffin. "That's why we were called."

The dragon rumbled and the Boffin picked up the baby. Then the dragon mother gently nudged the Boffin away.

"We have to take the baby away, apparently," the Boffin said.

The Mage nodded. "Yes, so it seems."

He laid his hand on the baby's head. "Hmm. He has a high destiny. Maybe a king."

"Queen, you mean," said the Boffin.

"Oh, yes. Silly me," said the Mage.

They climbed down from the nest and the dragon mother trumpeted. They were still enough dragon to understand that she was thanking them, and wishing them well. The Mage and the Boffin turned and did the head dipping gesture of thanks as well as they could in human form, then turned and walked back through the tunnel. Dragons scattered in all directions as they came out onto the ledge.

"How are we going to get her back?" wondered the Boffin. "We can't carry her when we are in dragon form, and it is impossible to walk from here. We need to get back to somewhere near where we arrived, otherwise we will be a long, long way from home when we step back."

"I have an idea," said the Mage. "I can shrink her to the size of a pea and then you can carry her in your crop. When we get near to the peak where we arrived, you can regurgitate her, and I'll expand her, and we can step back. Would that work?"

"Yes, that's a good plan. But what if she moves from my crop into my digestive system?"

"Oh, well, she wouldn't be digested, as she would be compressed, so you'd just poop her out."

"OK, undignified but safe. Let's do it."

So the Mage shrank the baby to the size of a pea and the Boffin swallowed her and stowed her in her crop. She flapped her wings. The Mage flapped his, and they tapped their snouts together then stepped over the edge of the ledge. The updraft caught them and tossed them high into the air. Their guide reappeared and led them southwards. Their escort of dragons formed up behind them.

The guide seemed playful and led them through narrow canyons and under overhangs, and through needle eyes in the rocks, causing their escort to split and single file and re-merge. The Boffin loved it and shrieked her joy. Even in the open the escort swirled and twisted in a loose cone centred on the guide dragon. It was an aerial symphony of joy. A murmuration of dragons.

At one point they encountered some herds of migrating beasts again, and again they stopped off and killed and ate a beast to build up their energy levels. Again the scavengers started to arrive before they had finished feasting.

As they got nearer to the point where they had stepped into this space, the escort dropped out one by one, so that eventually there were just the three of them.

They swooped down to tear up some of the tasty vegetation from another alpine meadow. The plants were reminiscent of heather, with dark berries and dark leaves, but the plants were tall and spindly, like many plants in this space of lower gravity.

Eventually, they arrived at a point where the guide dragon soared upwards and settled on a peak, just as the sun was setting to the west. Everything turned dimly pink as it was illuminated only by the halo. The brighter stars could be seen as the halo glow died down. The Boffin and the Mage settled beside their guide and the Boffin walked up to her and laid a hand on her snout.

"Thank you, my dear," she said "for your invaluable help. I salute you."

This was as close as she could come to expressing her feelings to the dragon while in human form. She hoped that it translated well to into dragon. The guide dragon snorted, which raised the surrounding dust. Then she raised her head and bugled.

"She says 'Thank you, on behalf of dragon kind'," said the Boffin. "Or something similar. It loses something in the translation."

The Mage nodded. "The baby?"

"Oh yes. I wasn't looking forward to this bit," she said.

She vomited on the ground. The Mage gestured and a pearl rose into the air, and he took it into the palm of his hand. He passed the other hand over it, and was suddenly holding the baby.

"Let's step across quickly," he said. "Her normal bodily functions will resume shortly."

They stepped across. Normal bodily functions were indeed resumed, which fortunately just left the Mage a little damp. He passed her over to the Boffin.

The baby started crying.

"What's wrong with her?" said the Mage worriedly.

"We've had all those kids, and you still can't speak baby," the Boffin laughed. "She's hungry. And a little tired, poor thing. Can you help please?"

"What? Oh, yes."

He gently touched the Boffin's breast, the Boffin somehow rearranged her clothing, and the baby attached herself to the Boffin's breast. They walked slowly home, the baby feeding happily. The Mage gestured with his hand, the shimmer that surrounded the house disappeared, and the Mage held the door open for the Boffin. Still holding the baby she relaxed into her seat with a sigh.

"Nappy," she said and the Mage hurried to look for some. Of course there weren't any. He checked that the Boffin wasn't watching, and reached through a fold in time to steal a couple of nappies from when they did have babies around.

"We'll put her in one of the boys' cots. I think we've still got one around." She knew exactly where the nappies had come from, of course.

"We're not going to keep her, are we?" asked the Mage nervously.

The Boffin considered pretending that she wanted to, then took pity on him.

"I was thinking of Queen Charlotte."

"Oh, yes, good idea," said the Mage.

Queen Charlotte was unable to have babies, and the Boffin was annoyed that she was unable to help the poor woman using her medicines or even her surgery. The Mage wasn't able to either, using his own special skills. This was the ideal solution.

King Edmund and Queen Charlotte were delighted to take the baby. So delighted that the Boffin warned them against spoiling her.

"We won't. I may not be able to have children, but my sister Irene has four, and they've grown up here at the Palace and are nice kids. I'm sure she'll help me out and let me know if she thinks that I'm doing something wrong. Coochie, coochie, coochie-coo!"

The Boffin assumed that the last bit was not directed at her.

"Charlie and Ed are both sensible people. They'll do OK," said Irene, "but I'm going to love being an Auntie!"

"One last thing," said the Mage. "She's dragon born, and her dragon nature will be suppressed for a long time, probably for sixty years or more, but will eventually come out. We don't know what this means yet, so we will check on her often after she turns sixty."

On the way home, with the horse clip-clopping along at a good rate, the Boffin snuggled up to the Mage.

"How long since we last had a baby, dear?"

"Well, Jimmy is fifty next year, and he's the last." He put his arm around her.

"Too soon to have another one, isn't it?"

"Yes," said the Mage, "but I couldn't stop you if you really wanted one."

The Boffin smiled at the way that the Mage's answer could be understood two ways.

"Don't worry dear. I don't want another baby," she said. "Yet."

***

The Quest

The Sons Set Out on a Quest

The Boffin's three sons came to her one day and announced that they wanted to go on a quest.

"Fine," she said, "and could you pick up some tomatoes from the shop on your way back?"

"Mum!!!" said the oldest brother disgustedly.

"What sort of quest were you thinking of?" asked their father, the Mage.

"Oh, I don't know. Something involving brave deeds and solving riddles. That sort of thing," said the eldest.

"So nothing involving tomatoes, then," said their Dad.

"Dad!!!"

"OK, OK."

He thought for a bit. "How about you go out and find the thing that you need the most?"

"What would that be?"

"That would be part of the quest," said the Boffin.

The three brothers looked at each other. That certainly had the air of a quest.

"OK," said the youngest son. "We'll do it!"

"I have one condition," said the Mage. "You have to wear these amulets. They will allow you to call us if you find yourselves in a situation that you can't handle or where you need our help. Don't be stupidly heroic, please. Your mother has crafted them, and I have put a charm on them so that you can't lose them. To make it a real quest, we won't be able to call you. You'll have to call us. OK?"

The three sons agreed to the condition and set off down the road. They walked through the town passing the shop as they went.

"Tomatoes!" said the oldest, disgustedly.

They soon reached open country and, like all siblings, started to bicker. Eventually they reached a crossroads and couldn't agree which way they should go, so they all started off in different directions. The youngest son went left, the oldest son went right, and, well, the middle son took the middle way.

The youngest son passed through some woods, then through a deep cutting and then through farmland. The eldest son passed through a deep cutting, then farmlands, and then some woods. The middle son passed through farmlands, then some woods and finally a deep cutting.

All three approached a cross roads and saw figures coming from two other directions. The three brothers met at the crossroads.

"Odd," said the oldest son. "Do you think that this is Mum and Dad's doing?"

The middle son waved his hand and a ball appeared on his palm. He studied it.

"No magic," he said, "so far as I can tell."

The youngest son produced a box with buttons on it. He pulled out an extending antenna and pressed a button.

"No science," he said, scanning the area, "so far as I can tell."

Back home the Boffin was laughing. The Mage came over to look. In her glass globe the boys were discussing the strange situation and in the end concluded that it was pure chance.

"Stop teasing them, dear. If they want to split up, let them."

"They're so easy to fool, and they don't know we're watching," said the Boffin.

At that moment the youngest son turned away from his brothers and looked straight at the Boffin and the Mage and winked.

"Well I never," said the Boffin.

The Mage laughed. "So much for not knowing that we are watching," he said. "Put away the globe, dear, and let them get on with it."

The Boffin sighed and put it away, but from time to time over the next few days she glanced longingly at the cupboard.

The boys walked down the road for a mile or two and came across another crossroad. They stopped and looked at it suspiciously. Finally, the oldest brother came to a decision.

"Luck!" he said, and the other two said the same, and they all bumped fists. Then once again the youngest son took the left-hand road, the oldest son took the right-hand road, and well, the middle son took the middle road.

The Quest of the Oldest Son

The oldest son found that he was getting hungry and tired. He was approaching a small town and decided to stay there the night. He thought of stopping off at the local Mystics chapel, but no one was around. Across the road lights had come on in the pastor's house, but he decided not to trouble her.

He had a little money, so he pressed on into the local town. He had a meal at the small pub, and then wondered where he was going to stay.

"No rooms," said the pub landlord. "It's market day today, and all accommodation will be full. You could try the castle.

The baron often lets people sleep in the stables. Are you on a Quest?"

The oldest son admitted that he was. He reflected that going on a quest seemed so grown up at home, but here it seemed a little silly.

"If so," continued the landlord, "the baron is looking for someone to get rid of a dragon. It's killed three people already and eaten two horses and some cows."

The oldest son thought that this was a bit odd. Dragons didn't usually hang around human space. His Mum and Dad had taken them to dragon space for a holiday a few times, and the dragons had been courteous, if a little standoffish. Dragon space had lighter gravity and many small moons. Their sun was surrounded by a pink halo, and the beaches were amazing rainbows of sands washed by the slow falling waves.

Something must be holding the dragon in human space, and he wondered what it was. No wonder the poor thing had been chomping on a few cows and horses. He wondered about the people. No doubt they had charged the dragon with raised swords to try to drive it off or something, so it was likely that the dragon killed them in self-defence.

He went up to the castle, which was a modest affair, surrounded by a wooden wall. All the doors in the wall were open, so times were peaceful, he supposed. He followed the smell of horses and the stable boy showed him a stall in which he could sleep. The stable boy gave him a bale of straw to make a bed.

"Are you here to kill the dragon?" asked the stable boy. "Have you got a sword?"

"No, I don't have a sword. But I might see if I can get rid of the dragon for the baron."

The stable boy snorted. "It'll eat you up," he said. "Anyway, come up to the house tomorrow morning and get some breakfast. Dad will be there and you can talk to him about the dragon."

"Your Dad is the baron?" he asked the stable boy.

"Yep, we're not like rich folks with lots of money," the boy laughed. "I hope you're not looking for a big reward! Because we're broke practically all the time."

The oldest son slept well and made his way up to the castle or house as the baron's son had called it. He went round the back and was invited into the kitchen and the baron's wife cooked him a big breakfast. The baron was a short cheerful looking man with wispy hair on the sides of his head.

"So you want to take on the dragon, or so my son tells me?" said the baron. "I'm a bit worried about sending you up there, to be honest. So we've lost a few sheep and cows, but they aren't worth a single life. But if you insist, my son will show you the way. How much do you want?"

"How much do I want?" repeated the oldest son, confused.

"If you get rid of the dragon. We don't have much money."

"Oh, if I can get rid of it for you, I don't want anything. I'll go up today and have a look, and see what the situation is." He didn't mention what he knew about dragons.

The baron nodded. "That's wise," he said. "The others who tried just went rushing in. Fools! I couldn't stop them."

The baron's son gave him directions. "I'd show you the way, but Dad needs me to do some stuff. I've been up there and the dragon pretty much keeps in the cave. If you are just going to have a look, it's pretty safe."

The oldest son thanked the baron and his son, and made his way towards a gate in the wooden wall.

"Just a minute," someone called.

He turned around and saw the most beautiful girl he had ever seen. She looked beautiful from the top of her auburn hair which was pulled back in a ponytail, down to her muddy gumboots. He found her oval face, her freckles, her work jacket with frayed sleeves and her well-worn blue jeans deeply attractive.

"Are you going to kill the dragon?" she said angrily.

"Not if I can help it," he said. "Dragons aren't usually vicious, and they don't usually stay around for long. They're noble animals."

"Oh." She relaxed. "Only, she's got eggs."

"She? Eggs? Really? Have you been in her cave?"

"Yes, though no one will believe me. She's got about half a dozen eggs. She showed me. And she sort of flickered."

"Like she was there one instant and not the next?"

"Yes!" The baron's daughter impulsively grabbed his hand. Her hands were as smooth as silk to his touch, though to honest, they would have felt silky to him if they were rough as sandpaper. They were white as snow against his darker skin. She took her hands back.

"I'm going up there to have a look today. Do you want to come too?" he asked.

She looked over her shoulder at the house.

"Come on then," she said, and they hurried through the gate.

"Dad won't mind. Mum might be a bit grumpy," she said.

"What's your name?" he asked.

"Sian," she replied.

"Really? So's mine. S-H-A-U-N." He laughed.

42

"Mine is spelled S-I-A-N," she said. "If you get rid of the dragon, Dad won't be able to pay you much. We're not very rich, even though Dad is a baron, and we live in a 'castle'."

"I'm not going to 'get rid' of the dragon. I'm going to see what is wrong, and I'm doing it for nothing. I feel sorry for the dragon."

"I'm glad. We've all got other jobs apart from the 'estate'. Mum works in the Mayor's office, and my brother and I work at the stables in town. I do the books for Dad, and we manage, but we can't afford a dragon removal bounty."

They climbed into the hills behind the castle and the town. Big boulders jutted from the grass and scree slopes fanned out from high above. They rounded a huge rock and turned into a grassy valley, and the cave was before them. They crept hand in hand up to the entrance, then Shaun clicked on a torch, and they walked slowly into the darkness.

The red light of the torch showed the dragon sitting on a few sticks and twigs which were a poor excuse for a nest. She saw them and rumbled a little. She moved aside to let them see her eggs.

"How did you see them before?" asked Shaun.

She clicked on her own torch and Shaun laughed gently.

"Sorry," he said.

The dragon stirred and disappeared and then came back again several times. It was like the flickering of an old movie or television screen. She appeared to be waiting.

"I think I know what's wrong. Don't be scared, I'm just going to see where she is going. OK?"

"OK, but don't be long."

Shaun stepped through to the dragon space. He quickly swung the light around. He was in a huge cavern with a pile of branches and sticks filling the bottom of it. That was more like it. The dragon popped in and popped out again. He stepped back.

Sian grabbed him and clung on.

"How did you do that? Where did you go?" she said.

She loosed her grip on him, but continued to hold his hand.

"Sorry," said Shaun. "It's just that there are other places, just like here. My Mum calls them 'spaces'. There's one where the dragons come from and that's where the mother dragon belongs. She must have stepped to here, and then had to lay her eggs here, and now she can't leave them. Poor thing. She can't carry them back. No hands."

"'Stepped'?"

"Any living thing can step between spaces, but some, like humans, don't instinctively know how to. We can carry her eggs back for her. Do you want to try?"

"Oh, yes, but I don't know how."

"Hold my hands. Step forward."

Suddenly they were in the dragon space next to the nest. Sian gasped.

"I feel different. Lighter."

"That's the gravity. It's different here. Can you take us back?"

"I think so," said Sian. "Ready, step!"

They were back with the mother dragon.

"I did it! But I don't know how! We can help her. We can carry her eggs back for her!"

They approached the first egg. They crouched down and linked hands at the bottom of the egg and stood up.

"To me, three, two, one, step," said Shaun.

They were next to the nest. They carefully climbed up the nest, balancing the egg between them, and carefully tipped it into the nest. The egg rolled down to the bottom of the nest.

"Hmm, that's not so good. The next egg will crash into the first."

They moved the first egg to one side, so that the next egg would roll past it, then they climbed down from the nest to the place where they had stepped over. Then they stepped back. The mother dragon was flickering back and forth between the dragon space and the human space.

"Next one," said Sian. "We can do this."

She was shaking and Shaun held her for a minute until she calmed down.

"OK," she said. "I'm OK. Let's do it."

They picked up the next egg and stepped to the dragon space. They carefully climbed up to the edge of the nest and tipped the egg over. It rolled down the slope and then took a kick off a stray twig and rolled off at an angle.

"Oh no, it's going to hit the other egg!" said Sian in horror.

The mother dragon flashed into the nest and stopped the rolling egg with her claw. She wagged her head and hissed.

"I think she's laughing," said Shaun, "but I'm not sure."

Sian and Shaun returned to the human space and slowly manhandled the rest of the eggs one by one to the dragon space and into the nest. Each time the mother dragon was there to catch the egg and guide it into a safe position. When the last egg was in place the dragon did a wriggling dance around the nest and trumpeted. It was deafening in the enclosed cave. Then she crouched down and lowered her head in front of the two humans, and finally settled down on the eggs, fussing them into place.

45

Shaun turned to Sian. "She's pleased. Do you want to see a little of this space? Dragon nests are usually high up, so it should be a good view."

They walked towards the opening of the cavern, and emerged onto a wide ledge high in a mountain range. In front of them smaller mountains marched steeply away in a way that would be impossible back in human space, down to a deep green sea. Foaming streams and creeks poured in leisurely fashion down the mountains to the broad valleys and into rivers that meandered slowly to the sea. The sun, as yellow as the human space sun, was high in the sky, surrounded by a pink halo. Ponderous clouds travelled slowly through the sky.

"It's wonderful!" said Sian. "Oh, look, there are other dragons! Did you know it would be like this?"

He nodded. "I've not seen it from so high up myself, as my Mum and Dad only took us to the beaches here. There were small dragons down there, bird sized ones. We called them 'seagulls'. We could see the big dragons flying high up between the mountains. So I had an idea that it would look like this."

"If humans can come here, why don't they? It's so beautiful."

"Not many people find it easy. Many have to practise for decades to do it even once. The first time I brought us across, I did all the work. When I asked you to take us back, I was surprised that you managed it right away. You are a special person."

"And you and your family? Are you special people too?"

Shaun looked at her. "My Mum and Dad are very special. My brothers and I are special. Sian, I like you a lot and hope to get to know you better, but my parents can scare people. Oh they're really nice, and I love them very much, but they are, as I said, very special, and that scares some people."

Sian slipped her arm round him. "I want to get to know you better too. I want to meet your family. Let's see if they scare me. Is it too soon to kiss?"

Shaun showed her that it wasn't too soon.

They walked back into the cave to the spot where they had stepped over. The mother dragon was asleep but opened one huge golden eye, sighed and closed it again. They stepped back together to the human space.

"We've vanquished the dragon," said Shaun ironically. "But what do we tell people?"

"You used a charm to scare it off? You burnt a chemical that it disliked and it flew off? You threw water on it and it crumbled to dust?" she joked.

"I like the chemical one. I'll use that. People like physical solutions these days."

A few days later he walked in the door at home. The Boffin was pleased to see her oldest son back from his quest.

He kissed her and said "Mum, I'm going to be working for a baron about a day west of here."

"I think I know him," said the Mage from his chair. "His 'castle' is more like a fortified house, and the 'estate' has shrunk quite a bit from what it was. A nice bloke though. He refuses to charge his tenants market rates, and has helped a few of them to buy the farms that their families have farmed for generations."

"That's the one," agreed Shaun.

"So, did you find what you needed on your quest?" asked the Boffin.

Shaun nodded. "I think so, Mum. But part of finding what you need is to realise that what you need is not fixed, and changes from time to time. I think I've found what I need at the moment, though."

The Boffin asked "Can you tell us her name, then?"

Her oldest son said "Mum!!!" and blushed furiously.

"My dear," said the Mage reprovingly. "Don't tease."

"Just a lucky guess," said the Boffin lightly.

The Middle Son Finds His Way

The middle son's name was Drew. He didn't much like his name as he had to keep explaining to people that it was just "Drew" and not a shortened form of "Andrew". He walked along the road until he came to the city, and was amazed at vibrancy of it, and all the bright people who lived there.

He soon got a job, plastering up advertisements on panels and billboards all over the city, though he had to pretend to be older than his fifteen years to get it. He shared a flat with three other boys who were a bit older than him, and set about enjoying the city. He made friends, he went to shows, and visited all the good restaurants, and the bad ones. He tried drinking, but didn't like it much and something in him prevented him from experimenting with drugs.

One day he was passing the theatre and saw a "help wanted" sign, and went in. At first, he saw no one, and then through an open door he saw a boy of about seventeen or eighteen sitting at a mirror removing make-up. The boy was wearing trousers with a thick black and white stripe, and a dark blue jacket with gold buttons.

Drew watched the boy taking off his make-up, fascinated by the process. Suddenly the boy stopped and spun round.

"What are you doing, matey, spying on me like that?"

"Sorry, there's a notice outside about a job. I wasn't spying. I was just interested."

"Norm!" the boy suddenly yelled. "Norm, where are you? We have an intruder."

An older man came into the room.

"What's all the shouting about? Oh, hullo. What can we do for you, son?"

"He's here for a job," said the boy with the make-up.

The older man, Drew judged him to be thirty or more, took him into another office.

"Welcome, sit down, please. Now what attracts you to this madhouse?" said Norm. "All we can offer is backbreaking work for little pay. What's your name? How old are you?"

"My name's Drew. I'm seventeen. I like the idea of working in the theatre. Is it really a madhouse?"

"Crazy, my dear Drew," said Norm. "How old are you again? You look fifteen tops. Have you run away from somewhere?"

Drew admitted he was really fifteen. "I've not run away. I'm on a quest to find the thing that I need the most."

It sounded silly immediately he said it, but Norm merely sniffed and said "Quests? Over-rated".

"OK, Drew, the job is to help out at the theatre, pretty much doing what needs doing. Sweeping, tidying, finding things. We're always losing things. Help with wardrobe, help with the stage wrangling, help with lighting. Help with make-up, help with anything. You can call yourself 'Backstage Manager' if you like. We'll pay you...."

Norm mentioned an incredibly low sum of money. "Well, that doesn't seem to have put you off," he commented when Drew didn't react.

"Can you start tomorrow? I don't open the theatre up until 11 in the morning, but I'll give you a key if you want."

Norm waved a key in the air, then he rummaged in a drawer. After retrieving several keys and comparing them and tossing them back he found a key that matched and handed it over.

"Are you the boss, sir?" asked Drew.

Norm looked at him. "Yes, but don't call me 'boss'. Or 'sir'. I own this heap of rotting timber and bricks. For my sins. Jason!"

The boy with the make-up stuck his head in the door. "What now?"

Norm sighed. "Show Drew where the brooms and things are," he said. "Please?"

"Come on then," said Jason, and disappeared.

He showed Drew a cupboard with a few battered brooms, mops and buckets. A stack of rat traps was tumbled at the back. Bottles of cleaning materials sat on the shelves and everything was covered with a thick layer of dust.

"It's about time we had someone to do the tidying up," said Jason.

He picked up a toilet plunger and fenced with an invisible enemy.

"What do I have to clean?" asked Drew.

"Everything," said Jason over his retreating shoulder.

The next day, Drew did a survey of the theatre. From the front of house, to the auditorium to the back of the stage, to the flies high in the roof, to the dressing rooms and offices and facilities. He considered. Apart from the front of house and the auditorium, everything was messy. The only areas backstage which were relatively clear were the passages to and from the dressing rooms, and the offices, swept relatively clean by the movement of people.

He thought for a bit and consulted his mental map. He'd do the areas that took the most traffic first and expand on that. He started sweeping the main passages, taking pains over the corners which had received no care for a long time. He was about two-thirds the way through when he found a chocolate wrapper for a brand which he knew hadn't existed for years. He was staring at it bemusedly when Norm came along.

"Oh, you've started. Good. I was afraid that you'd done a runner. Carry on. The cast will be arriving soon."

"Who looks after the front of house and the auditorium?" he asked.

"A couple of old ladies who've done it for years. I have nightmares where one of them dies. I'd have to get someone in at market rates!"

He absent-mindedly kissed Drew on the cheek and dashed off. Drew was surprised for a minute, but discovered that Norm did this with all the males working in the theatre. There was no doubt that Norm preferred boys to girls, but the kisses didn't seem to mean anything much. Drew decided to ignore it if it happened again, like everyone else.

The cast started to arrive. The aggressively male leading man shared a dressing room with Jason. They seemed to hate each other, but late one night Drew came across them sharing a bottle of wine quite amicably, so he wasn't sure what was going on there.

The leading girl was an ethereal blonde who shared her room with the other main female cast member who was a brunette with strong glasses. The blonde didn't so much walk from place to place but waft. Once she got on stage, though, she could act anything from the hero's sweetheart to a tough gangster's moll with ease. The brunette couldn't see without her glasses and had to be directed to the stage. The other actors helped her to move from place to place once she was on it. But she too could take any role and make it her own.

Norm was the only one who didn't share a dressing room, and that was because he used his office. On the other hand, the chorus, an assorted group of six girls who were both singers and dancers shared a dressing room the size of a cupboard and Drew got used to ignoring glimpses of various inadvertently displayed body parts.

The chorus consisted of girls of different body shapes from skinny to not so skinny. Their heights varied from tiny to willowy. They were used to performing as swans, policemen, showgirls, or even a Greek chorus. Their voices harmonised reasonably well, and they filled in odd roles such as "a maid" or "a passer-by" or even "a bear in the forest". They were the backbone of the company, and they were treated really badly. They didn't seem to mind.

When there was a performance Drew set up the properties table, and retrieved the properties when they were carried off-stage or at the end of a performance. Sometimes he had to hunt for them, as the cast tended to leave them almost anywhere.

He looked after the costume department too, washing them when they started to whiff, and mending them when they got torn. His mother would have been surprised. No, astounded!

Now and then he stood in on stage if the company was short of a messenger, or a centurion, or a farmer. If the prompt boy was sick he sat in a little box under the front of the stage, with the script, feeding the lines if anyone forgot them.

He loved the life, and moved to an apartment closer to the theatre. He completely cleaned up and tidied up the theatre. His props were immaculate, over time his costumes were impressive. He started to dress like his fellows at the theatre. His clothes became brighter and more outgoing, unlike his previously more usual anonymous browns, greens and greys.

One day he was leaving the theatre early in the morning after tidying up after a performance. He locked the theatre door, and walked down the alleyway to the main road. Several lads were loitering around the entrance to the alleyway.

"There's one," said one of them. They were all close-cropped, while Drew had let his hair grow long. The lads all wore t-shirts, short legged blue jeans with large black boots. They were all tattooed on arms, legs and faces.

They closed in around Drew as he walked down the alleyway.

"Where do you think are you going?"

"Home. Let me through, guys."

Someone punched him on the ear and as he turned they hit him in the mouth, splitting his lip. Someone tripped him and he fell onto his back. He was kicked in the head, and then someone kicked him in the stomach and in the back.

"Hey! What's going on?" someone shouted.

He rolled up in a ball, and they stopped kicking him. He heard various cries and thumps as a fight went on above him. A face appeared in front of him as he lay there. One of the punks. He was bleeding from the nose. Someone pulled the punk up out of his line of sight.

"Let's get out of here!" said someone in a panic.

Everything went quiet. Then Norm's face appeared in front of him.

"Let's get you back inside, chook," he said.

Norm half carried him back inside the theatre and settled him on the couch in his office.

"I saw those guys earlier, so I hung around. Sorry I didn't get there quick enough. Let's get you to hospital."

"No!" said Drew jerking upright before sinking back. He pulled his amulet from around his neck and pressed the jewel.

Instantly the Boffin appeared in the room.

"Holy ghost!" said Norm.

"Not quite," said the Boffin. "I'll explain later. What's been going on here?"

She checked out her son, and ran one of her instruments up and down him.

"Hmm, mostly superficial. Kidney is bruised. You'll be pissing blood for a day or so, but that's all, fortunately. Mild brain contusion. It'll fix itself. Cut above the eyebrow. I'll stitch that. Split lip. Some bruises."

"Mum, can we go home? I'd like to see Dad. I want to come back here, but I think my quest is over."

"Sure. Want to come?" she asked Norm.

Norm nodded, and suddenly they were home, in the Boffin and the Mage's kitchen.

Norm sat down heavily on a chair.

"Wow!" he said. "I was expecting you to call a cab. How did you do that? Am I dreaming?"

"Sorry, I'll explain later, but you're going to forget all this when we take you back," said the Boffin.

Norm nodded. "That's fine by me. It's pretty scary. Who are you people?"

The Mage, who was looking a little startled himself, said "You're actually taking it really well. What's happened here?"

"Oh, I noticed some punks hanging around, so I stayed nearby. Drew came out, and they jumped him, and I wasn't quick enough to stop them. Sorry, Drew."

"S'OK, Norm" said Drew, drowsily, "How did you manage to handle them? There were, what, four of them?"

"My big secret, lovely boy. I was in the Army. Special Services. Those punks didn't stand a chance, really."

"Thanks, pal," said Drew. "Stitch me up, Mum. I need to sleep I think."

When Drew had been patched up and sent to bed, the Boffin said "We're really grateful to you, Norm, for what you did. We could have patched up pretty much any injury, but if they'd killed him..."

Norm said "No worries. I love the little so-and-so. He's like the son I can never have."

The Mage laughed and clapped him on the shoulder. He felt Norm's future.

"You know, Norm, I can see that you are lonely, but I think that there's someone out there for you, somewhere," said the Mage.

Norm laughed. "Better late than never I suppose. Do you want to take me back now? I'll leave Drew in your capable hands for now. I hope he comes back to the theatre."

The next day Drew woke up.

"Where's Norm?"

"We took him back, dear. He hopes you'll go back when you are better. What do you think?"

"Yeah, definitely, I'll go back. I was so happy there. But I think that my quest is over. 'What I need the most?' It changes all the time. One minute I need friends. Then I need a job. Then I need something that I enjoy. And all the time I need family. There's never any one thing."

He coughed. "Ouch! Why didn't my amulet protect me?" he wondered.

"Oh, it did. It got Norm to hang around."

"Hmm, that'll do as a working hypothesis," he said thoughtfully, teasing his mother with one of her favourite sayings.

The Youngest Son meets a Gremlin

None of the Mage and the Boffin's sons were unintelligent. In fact, they were brighter than most, but the youngest son was the brightest of the three. He'd deduced that they were being watched well before his brothers did, and what is more he'd worked out how.

When they reached the second crossroads and met up again, his scan did indeed show no science, just as his brother's scan showed no magic. But he knew how his parents had done that too, and showed them that he knew it with a wink.

As he wasn't a silly lad he left the Mage and Boffin's protection stuff in place. After all, he might be in dire need of the protection at some time. He was only twelve years old, and he knew that there were plenty of things that he would not be able to handle by himself.

However, he was happy as he walked along his branch of the road. It was nice to get out by himself. He loved his brothers but sometimes felt overshadowed by them. He was passed by a few cars steaming down the road and wondered if he should thumb a lift. No, he'd do it the hard way. He continued walking.

The sun sank lower in the sky, and he thought about stopping for the night. In the end he just hopped over a hedge and picked a grassy spot away from the crops in the field. He opened a flap of his backpack and removed a silver pearl. He held it in the palm of his hand and passed the other hand over it, and he was holding a lightweight tent.

He set up the tent and then cooked his meal over a small stove that he also popped out of a silver pearl. He wondered whether his brothers had packed any camping gear, and smiled. Probably not. He sat and watched the stars wheeling slowly in the sky until the moon came up and blotted most of them out. An owl sat in a nearby tree and regarded him curiously, then flew silently away. A hedgehog snuffled past. The youngest son popped out his sleeping bag and slept soundly in his small tent.

In the morning he cooked an oatmeal porridge. He was just halfway through eating it when he realised that he was being watched. A young girl was seated cross-legged on the other side of the stove. He'd not noticed her arrive.

"I hate oatmeal, me," she said. "Got any bacon?"

"No!" he said surprised. "Where did you come from?"

"Farm," she said gesturing over her shoulder. "I get out early, or they give me work to do."

She was smaller than him, but probably around his age, he decided. She had dark ebony skin, darker even than his own dark skin, and had curly black hair much like his. When she grinned, which was most of the time, her teeth showed bright white. She wore a t-shirt which was meant for someone much larger and which was printed with a cartoon of a stylised rodent, and jeans cut off to shorts. Her shoes were sneakers that had seen better days.

"What's your name?" she asked. "I'm Susan, but they always call me Gremlin."

She flashed him what she intended to be an evil grin.

"Hullo, Gremlin. I'm Cam. What do you do, Gremlin, when you aren't bumming breakfast off strangers."

She shrugged. "Stuff. Farm work if I can't get away from Uncle. Cooking with Auntie if I'm lucky. School sometimes, but they are nasty to me there. Just stuff."

"Stuff that doesn't involve washing it seems."

She jumped up. "You're mean! Just like the rest of them."

Tears streamed down her dirty face.

He jumped up too. "I'm sorry. That **was** mean of me. I apologise. I'm used to fighting with my big brothers."

She sat down again. "OK."

"The waterworks switched off pretty quickly."

"Yeah, it's a trick. I was annoyed though. On the farm we don't have tap water and washing in the trough is pretty stink."

"Really?"

"No, I just made that up."

"Are you naturally annoying or is it a lifestyle choice, Gremlin?"

She grinned at him. "Come and meet my family. They'll give you a job, even if you are a tramp."

"A tramp? At least I shower now and then."

"So do I. Fell in the pigpen on the way here."

"Is that true?"

She just laughed. Cam packed up his camp, which wasn't made easy by Gremlin who wanted to look at everything. He had to use misdirection to shrink his stuff down to pearls. He slung his backpack on and followed her to the farm.

"How'd you do that pearl thing?" she asked.

"You spotted that? Rats!"

"Can't trick a trickster."

"Sorry, I can't tell you that."

"OK. I'll find out eventually."

"No you won't."

"Yes I will," she said confidently.

They arrived at the farm. Cam wouldn't have been surprised if Gremlin had introduced her parents, but no, he was introduced to her aunt and uncle. The farmhouse was clean and relatively tidy, and her aunt and uncle both had the same dark skin and curly hair as Gremlin. When her aunt saw how dirty she was, she sent Gremlin off to the shower.

"And put some decent clothes on," her aunt called after her.

"We buy her good clothes, but she insists on wearing that t-shirt and those awful shoes, most of the time."

"So you want a job on the farm, do you? You're a bit young. What are you, twelve?" asked the uncle.

"That was Gremlin's idea, but yes, it's a good one. I'll do anything, well, anything I can manage. Perhaps you'd like to look at this letter from my parents, sir."

He passed over the paper, but the uncle shoved it over to his wife.

"Sorry son, I can't read. Something up here won't let me learn, the doctors said." He tapped his head. He didn't seem worried.

"Your mother has given us contact information if we need it. She says it's OK for you to travel by yourself. You're on a quest. Well I never!" said Gremlin's auntie. "We can put him in Jim's room."

Cam came to call them Uncle and Auntie just like Gremlin. Uncle and Auntie had five sons and Jim, the middle son was away at university. The farm was a moderate size and with four sons and Uncle, and with Cam's help and Gremlin's help no one was too overworked.

Gremlin's help was often worse than no help at all, though. Her main chore was the pigs and Cam was assigned to help her, most days. Mucking them out often ended with them both covered in pig poo. Or Cam drenched by the hose. He watched Gremlin closely and was fairly sure she wasn't doing it on purpose. But he wasn't certain.

Gremlin found out about the quest.

"What's that all about?" she asked. They had taken a break from the pig poo and Gremlin was about three or four metres up an oak tree. Cam was sitting at the bottom praying that she didn't slip or break a branch. There was a sudden crack.

"Oops. Good job I didn't put my weight on that branch."

She shinned down the tree.

"Well?"

"It was my brothers' idea. I thought it was a bit silly actually, but it sounded fun."

"Is it? I bet they're rescuing princesses and becoming famous. And you're mucking out pigs."

"Yeah," he said, chewing on a bit of grass. "I don't mind. I like it. But I might be going home soon. School is starting soon. Was it true about you being bullied at school?"

"Sort of," she said. "They teased me at first. Then they didn't."

She looked at a beetle crawling up a grass stem.

"Hmmm?" Cam said.

"Nothing like that!" protested Gremlin, though Cam wondered what she was denying. "I think that Auntie had a word with the teacher. When Auntie 'has a word', things happen".

"Gremlin, can I ask, what happened to your Mum and Dad? You don't have to answer."

"No, it's all right. I don't remember them much. I was too small. Mum was Auntie's sister, and Dad was from a farm down the road. When Mum and Dad got married he came to live with Auntie and Uncle. Something about his parents not approving."

"Mum had me and then caught the flu and died. Medicines didn't help. Dad went crazy for a while, I think, but then he was getting better. I just remember him playing with me on the big carpet."

She paused and thought.

"Then me Dad was found in the river, tangled with some roots. He'd been clearing the bank and cutting back the willows. He'd slipped and fallen in and got caught by the roots. Some people said he'd killed himself, but it didn't make sense. Why do it that way? And there were marks on the bank. Auntie 'had a word' and the rumours stopped."

Cam was silent for a bit.

"You're wondering if the story was true," said Gremlin. "Or if it was another of my tall stories."

She seemed hurt. Cam looked at her.

"I don't think it was a story. I wasn't wondering that. I was wondering how losing my Dad and Mum would have affected me."

Gremlin burst into tears. "Thanks for believing me," she said. Gremlin crying for real was a lot different from Gremlin putting it on. He didn't know what to do, so he patted her shoulder.

"I have a cry like that every once in a while," she said. "Then I'm all right. Anyway, let's go and see if there are conkers on the Horse Chestnut tree!"

"Wrong season," said Cam, but she was off and running. He sighed, and got up and followed her.

That evening after the evening meal he was helping Auntie with the washing up.

"I have to go home," he said. "It's been a while."

"Noooo! Not so soooon!" said Gremlin. "We've been having fun! You can't go!"

She ran up and started pummelling him.

"That's enough!" said Auntie, quite mildly. Gremlin stopped, but she was still crying.

"It's not fair," she said. About nothing in particular.

"In the morning?" asked Auntie.

"Yes, I think so. It will take me all day to get home, so I'd better start early."

Gremlin rushed off crying. Cam went to follow her, but Auntie gestured for him to stay there.

"Thanks for your help, son," said Uncle. "You've been a great help."

"With the pigs?" asked Cam, puzzled. He hadn't done an awful lot, if he thought about it.

"With Gremlin. She gets a bit bored, and if she gets bored, she gets silly, and if she gets silly, accidents sometimes happen."

"Remember when she fell through the roof of the chicken shed?" reminisced Auntie. "Of course we should have spotted that it was going rotten. Chickens and straw and bits of roof everywhere! No eggs for two days."

She turned to Cam. "Don't worry, Cam. I'll talk to her later. I'll make you some sandwiches for your journey."

The next morning, Cam woke up early. He went downstairs and Auntie made him breakfast.

"Gremlin's already gone out," said Auntie. "She's calmed down a bit. If you go out by the pig sty she might be there."

"Thanks Auntie. Thanks for everything," said Cam and gave her a hug, picked up his backpack and left.

He went out by the sty. Gremlin wasn't there, but the sty was as spotlessly clean as a sty could be. The pigs had been fed and were lying contentedly on the straw. He looked around a bit and then decided that he needed to get a move on. As he walked towards the road, Gremlin slid down from the roof unseen and watched him go. She sniffed. Then she sniffed again.

Cam walked along the road towards home in two minds. He had enjoyed living with Gremlin's family. True, Gremlin was annoying and irritating, but she was also interesting and fun to be with. He was still looking forward to getting home, telling his parents about his 'quest', and finding out how his brothers had done. He was happy with what he had achieved, even though it didn't amount to much, really.

He got to the point where the brothers had parted, and because his mother had been teasing them on the way out, he wasn't sure of the way home. He pulled an instrument from his backpack and scanned all three roads and started down the one that his instrument had told him was the correct one. Then he frowned and paused. He pulled out his instrument again and looked at it. At extreme range it showed someone behind him, just behind the dry stone wall around a field.

He walked a little further down the road and the person behind him followed him behind the wall. He turned and looked back. No one. Uh-oh. He carried on at the speed that he had been travelling before, until he reached a point where there was a gate, set back a little from the road. The stone walls and the gate formed a small rectangle. He ducked into the space and waited. Someone came crashing along on the field side, detouring further into the field to pass the gate.

"Gremlin!" he cried. "I knew it was you." She shrieked and then swore.

"That's not very nice," he said. "What are you doing, following me? What about your Auntie and Uncle?"

Gremlin started sobbing as she climbed over the gate.

"You're angry! It was such fun having you there, I wanted to come with you. I left a note for Auntie. She won't mind."

"Of course she'll mind! What were you thinking?"

"Auntie and Uncle are nice and so are my cousins, but I'm the odd one out."

"Oh, Gremlin, you're not the odd one out! They love you. All of them."

"What am I going to do?" she wailed. "They're going to h-h-hate me!"

"I doubt that!" he said, giving her a hug. "Anyway, let's carry on to our house. It's not far. Then we can see what we can do to sort out this mess. Mum's good at that sort of thing. Oh, Gremlin!"

"I know, I know, I'm stupid, aren't I?"

They walked up the road towards Cam's home, with Gremlin criticising herself at every step. Eventually Cam stopped dead.

"Gremlin, will you stop! We'll sort this out. What's the worst that could happen?"

"Your Mum could throw me out. My Auntie and Uncle could throw me out. I'd not have a h-h-h-home!"

"Gremlin! Now you are being ridiculous. Firstly my Mum wouldn't throw you out and secondly your Auntie and Uncle both love you. They'd definitely not throw you out."

Gremlin blew her nose noisily. "I know. You are right of course. I'm silly, aren't I? I'm behaving like I'm five or something."

"Irritating, maybe. Annoying, maybe. But silly? No. If I know my Mum, I'm going to get blamed."

They wandered on and eventually reached Cam's home. Cam practically had to pull Gremlin through the door.

"Mum, I'm home," he called. "And I've got a surprise."

The Boffin came in from the kitchen closely followed by the Mage. The Boffin rushed up to her son and kissed him.

"Who's this?" she asked.

"Some urchin I found on the road, Mum."

"Cam," wailed Gremlin.

"Mum, this is Gremlin. I've been working on her Uncle's farm for the last few weeks. She followed me home."

"Cam," wailed Gremlin again.

"Stop teasing her, Cam. It's not funny."

"Well, you did!" said Cam to Gremlin.

"No I didn't. Well, yes, I did."

"You're welcome here, my dear, but I sense that there's some problem. Did you run away from your Auntie and Uncle, dear?"

Gremlin gulped. "Yes, sort of. I was just following Cam."

"I can't imagine why. He's nothing to write home about." Cam snorted.

"We had such fun. I didn't want it to stop. Am I silly?"

"No dear," said the Mage. "Just a little impetuous. Like others that I know," he said looking at the Boffin.

"Yes, well," said the Boffin, elbowing her spouse gently in the midriff, "Anyway, you're welcome, Gremlin, dear. We can sort this out."

She hugged the girl and gave her a handkerchief to blow her nose.

"Thanks," said Gremlin. "Thank you."

She hugged the Boffin back.

Later the Mage came up behind the Boffin and put his arm around her. She turned her face up for a kiss. He obliged.

"You're thinking of us, many years ago," he stated.

The Boffin listened to Cam and Gremlin bickering in the sitting room. She sighed.

"Yes. It's been so long. And we were a lot older when we met."

"Do you regret it?"

"No, not an instant of it."

"Same here. Why do they remind you of us? We never argued, did we?"

66

"No, my love, we never have. But there's something. Can we hand the baton on, perhaps?"

"Cam's the ultimate Boffin, but he understands that magic has a power. Do you see her as the Mage? She's certainly all feeling and emotion. A little raw perhaps. No control."

"Maybe. Just maybe. Early days yet. Anyway, she's one of yours. Definitely."

"I wonder what it is like to grow old?" he said. "You know, we have this discussion every hundred years or so, don't we?"

"We'll find out some time. Maybe this time, maybe not."

The next day the Mage and the Boffin, with Cam and Gremlin, took a trip to Gremlin's home. Their car took only a couple of hours to complete the journey even with a stop to top up the water and to burn some more wood to build up the steam pressure.

Gremlin's Auntie and Uncle hugged Gremlin until she was short of breath.

"You've given us such a fright," said Auntie, kissing her. "What have you been up to?"

"Oh Auntie, I'm sorry. I was silly. I was having so much fun with Cam that I wanted it to carry on."

"Silly girl!" said Auntie.

"Well," said the Boffin, "we don't mind having her with us for a while, if that's OK with you. She could go to school with Cam, since she's the same age, more or less. How about we send them back to you in the holidays?"

Auntie looked at her. "Let's take a walk, just the two of us," she suggested.

The Boffin and Auntie took a walk outside. They looked at each other.

"Don't I know you from somewhere?" asked Auntie.

The Boffin considered. Should she suggest Auntie look in the mirror? True, they had different skin colours, different hair and even different body shapes, but Auntie might have the eyes to see.

"I don't think so," said the Boffin eventually. "But I've got relatives over this way."

Auntie returned to the topic of Cam and Gremlin.

"Me and Uncle have been together since we were kids. We weren't a couple until we were fifteen, sixteen. We got married at eighteen. You think that Gremlin and Cam are the same? I've been wondering myself."

"Yes, we think that they may be. I'm almost certain. We were older when I met my husband, but we married as soon as we could, and have rarely been apart."

Auntie nodded. "OK. You have her for the term, and we'll have her back in the holidays. Send Cam too, of course. Agreed?"

"Of course. Agreed."

So Gremlin came to live with the Mage and the Boffin and Auntie and Uncle watched them all go off in the car. She said to Uncle "I'm sure I know her. I'm certain. But where....?"

One day Cam came in and saw the Mage teaching Gremlin how to compress things to a pearl.

She smirked and said "Told you so!"

Cam was both annoyed at her and pleased for her, which confused him. He went in search of his mother, and asked her why.

"How did your Quest go?" asked the Boffin.

"Quest? What's that to do with anything? What did I need the most? Well, that changes all the time, of course. There's not one single thing."

He thought a bit. "Well, I've been the youngest brother all my life. My brothers have always looked after me. Gremlin's sort of like a younger sister to me. I'm always looking out for her. Maybe that's what I need at the moment?"

The Boffin nodded, a bit sadly. Soon her baby was going to grow up. When she touched Gremlin or Cam she could feel the bond between them so strongly that she knew that it was for life. It was a bitter-sweet sensation for her. One that she'd had many times in her life.

The End of the Quest

The three brothers were gathered round the table at home. Sian happened to be visiting, and she and Gremlin were out walking somewhere. The Mage and the Boffin had gone to the market shopping.

"I hear that you 'slew a dragon', Shaun," said Drew.

"Yeah, that's what people say. It's silly really. You've heard the real story of course?"

"Sian told us," said Cam. "She's nice."

Shaun nodded. "Yeah, I know."

He turned to his brother. "I like Gremlin. She's funny."

"I know," said Cam. "She's a great kid."

His older brothers looked at each other and Shaun raised his eyebrows. Drew nearly laughed but suppressed it.

"What about you, Drew? Got any girl friends?" said Shaun.

"One or two," said Drew. He wasn't going to give anything away. As second brother he was always looking for an advantage over his big brother.

Shaun was disappointed. "What about the Quest?" he said.

"'The thing that you need the most.' That's what we were looking for, wasn't it?"

"It changes all time, doesn't it. It can be more than one thing," said Shaun. "I'd say Sian at the moment. If we stay together, as I think we will, then what? A home? A career? A family? All three? At this point I don't know. But when the time comes, I'll know, I think."

"I'd say Gremlin," said Cam.

His brothers looked at him and he blushed.

"What? She's just a pal!"

His brothers just smiled.

Drew said "At the moment, I'd say the theatre. I get so much joy out of it. I've not met the girl yet who means more to me than the theatre, but I think that I probably will. I'll always love the theatre though. Does that sound silly?"

Shaun and Cam shook their heads.

"Quest over?" asked Shaun.

"Quest over," agreed Cam and Drew.

"You know," said Cam. "I realised when I was coming back home that we'd rarely been away from Mum and Dad before. I was pleased that I'd managed OK by myself."

"Me too," said Shaun. "I'm glad I was able to help out that dragon. And the baron."

"I'm the odd one out again," said Drew. "I had to call Mum in, and I didn't bring back a girl, like you two lover boys."

The Boffin had just returned home and heard the last bit.

"You all did really well," she said. "Drew, it wasn't your fault that you got jumped by a bunch of punks. Norm was raving about the brilliant job you were doing at the theatre."

"Actually, guys, Dad and I were wondering when you were going to stretch your wings a little. We thought of forcing the issue, but decided to let things happen naturally, and they did. One thing though — you didn't bring back any tomatoes."

***

The Forgetting

In the beginning two titanic empires fought for control of the world, of mankind. One empire was founded on the rock of magic, while the other was founded principle of science.

The Empire of Science built large machines that crawled across the surface of the world, causing death and destruction everywhere they went. The Empire of Magic created balls of fire which scorched the earth and destroyed the large machines of the Empire of Science.

The Empire of Magic sensed an opening and attacked the factories where the machines were being made. In retaliation the Empire of Science targeted the places where the Empire of Magic was weaving its curses and its spells.

And so the conflict escalated, and the people sheltered in caves and vaults underground, while up above the factories of the Empire of Science still produced the clothes, the furniture, and the other goods that people could no longer buy.

The Empire of Magic had no audience for its plays and shows, its love potions and its medicines, its spells and its cures. The war had driven people underground, and they starved and died and lived in fear.

One day a young man named Simon climbed out of the basement, where he had been hiding and starving, and searched for food on the surface, in spite of the danger. He filled his bags with as many tins as he could and walked back to his hole in the ground. Just as he was about to duck out of sight a machine of the Empire of Science spotted the movement and a charm of the Empire of Magic also noticed him.

Both weapons hit him at the same time and knocked him sideways through all the many spaces that are a step away. He arrived rather shaken in a space where the dark was light and the light was dark. Grey shapes slithered over grey rocks and slid into and out of a grey sea. The only colour was the golden glow that surrounded him.

"THIS STOPS NOW!!!!" he shouted, and the grey shapes slithered away or dived into the grey sea.

Simon stepped back to human space and raised his hands. A pulse of gold spread out from him into the distance. All the machines stopped and the curses and spells tumbled from the sky and rolled to a stop. The golden glow still surrounded him, and he sat on a rock and waited.

When the representatives of the Empire of Science reached him, he said "Bring me the Chief Scientist."

When the representatives of the Empire of Magic appeared, he said "Bring me the High Wizard."

Of course, they did not come alone. The Chief scientist brought along his most trusted aides and as much scientific equipment as they could manage. They directed their instruments at Simon and tut-tutted at the results.

"If I could just take a sample of your blood, please, sir," said one of the medical scientists moving forward. Simon gestured and he stopped frozen to the spot.

"I said 'THIS STOPS NOW'", said Simon. "Chief Scientist, what do you think of Magic?"

"Stuff and nonsense, of course. Silly superstition that should be routed out!" answered the Chief Scientist and most of the other scientists nodded in agreement.

"Really? Then it would surprise you then that your gunners cross their fingers before they load their big guns. That the riflemen kiss a bullet before they load it. That many of them carry a small round pebble for luck. If you believe that Magic and superstition should be routed out, move to the left."

Most of the delegation moved to the left, leaving only four of the younger scientists shaking in front of Simon. Simon turned to those on the left.

"Your blind bigotry has devastated the world. You are banished to a space where only Science exists. Where there is no Magic. When you get tired of a space without Magic, you merely have to express your regret and you will return to our human space."

Simon gestured and the group of scientists on the left vanished. He gestured to the four remaining scientists to come closer.

"You are now the representatives of Science in human space. Do you have a preference for your leader?"

They looked at one another and mutually selected one of the two young ladies, one with a dark skin, dark eyes, and dark hair.

"I'd be honoured to be the representative of Science," she said, "and I certainly am not in favour of routing out Magic. I believe that there should be a balance between the two."

Simon put his hand on her shoulder and the golden glow momentarily expanded to include her.

"I hope that you don't regret that decision, my dear. Please stand by me."

He gestured. "Now you have control of your machines back. I suggest that you remove them and maybe dismantle them, but it is up to you. Please, return to your laboratories and my thanks to you."

The High Wizard also brought a delegation.

"I demand that you release our curses and spells. We need them to defeat the evil scientists."

"What do you think of Science, High Wizard. Is it really evil?" said Simon.

"Of course it is! It denies the reality of Magic, and strives to force all things into its abominable straight-jacket."

"So do you measure the ingredients of your spells and potions or do you just guess? Do your junior wizards experiment with new spells or variations of old spells?"

The High Wizard spluttered a bit.

"All those of you who think that Science is evil, please move right."

Once again, only five nervous youngsters were left in the centre. Simon turned to the group on the right.

"You want a world where Science has been banished. Well, I banish you to a space where there is no Science. If you find that you miss Science, as I suspect you will, you merely have to say so, and you will return."

He gestured and the delegation disappeared.

"I want you to pick a leader," he told the remaining five. "A representative of the Magic practitioners."

They chose a young man, whose skin was olive rather than dark. He had sparkling brown eyes.

"I'm honoured, sir," he said.

"Please come and stand with me," said Simon. "The rest of you, please return to your studies, and please tidy up your curses and spells. They will only cause problems if they are left lying around and people stumble on them."

He gestured and released the curses and spells. The remaining wizards left.

Simon turned to the new leader of the Magic delegation.

"I hope that you don't regret your elevation," he said, and laid his hand on the young man's shoulder. His golden glow briefly extended to include the young wizard.

"My friends, we have a big task ahead of us," he said. "I can see some problems to come, but not the solutions. Such is life. You, sire, will be my Mage, and you, ma'am, will be my Boffin. Can we join hands, please? Interestingly you are not the first, and you will not be the last."

They joined hands.

Simon said "The weapons that hit me gave me such power! But it was just mine to give away. You, sir, and you, ma'am, are the recipients of this charge. Do only good with it, please, for the world's sake. Your first challenge will be soon, but I will give you a week to get to know each other, and then we will start work. Magic and Science will wax and wane in influence, but neither will ever completely dominate or disappear. Now!"

Simon's golden aura flowed out of him and into the two young people. Simon sighed and collapsed. The new Mage just caught him as he fell.

The Mage looked at the new Boffin. "He's just passed out. I think that he thinks that he gave us all his power, but a tiny bit remains. He's going to be a great king, I think. He can't escape his destiny. None of us can."

"He'll need our help," said the Boffin. "What did he mean, he would give us a week to get to know each other?"

The human space faded out, and they found themselves on a beach. The sand was white with bluish swirls. The vegetation that backed the beach was dark green with a bluish tinge. The sun was much like the human space sun and was high in the sky.

"Oh, it's beautiful! Are we here for a week then?"

"Let's try," said the Mage. He stepped forward and frowned. Then he stepped forward again.

The Boffin was laughing at him. "Are you so eager to get away from me?" she asked.

The Mage realised what he'd done. "Oh, sorry, no, of course not."

The Boffin was still laughing at him when she turned around. "Oh. Look!"

Behind them was a small cabin. The Boffin ran up and in through the open door.

"Wow! Everything we might need."

She dashed through into one of the two bedrooms. "Oh, boy's stuff. Yours!"

She dashed into the other. "That's more like it. Yeah, swimming togs."

In a few minutes, she came out of her room dressed in a bikini. The Mage gulped. She didn't seem to notice, but dashed out of the cabin into the surf.

The Mage hurried to change and soon they were splashing about, dunking each other and having a wonderful time. Eventually they tired and headed back to the cabin. The Boffin changed into a floral dress that wrapped around her, while the Mage changed into a t-shirt and shorts.

"Hmm," said the Boffin, fiddling with a chrome and glass box on the kitchen bench. "An automatic oven or something."

She pulled a menu card out of it. "What do you fancy?"

They selected their meals and entered the codes for them into the oven. When it pinged they brought out their meals and sat down, only for the Mage to jump up and look in the fridge.

"Wine?"

"Yes please, something aromatic, please."

They chatted over their meals and wine, and discovered that each was interested in the other's field of expertise, even though officially they were supposed to hate it. They showed each other their favourite tricks.

"Mmmm," said the Mage, "I've a feeling that this space was made by Simon for us, and won't exist after we leave."

"There are others almost as good," said the Boffin, reaching out to hold his hand. "Have you been to dragon space?"

"No, you will have to take me there," said the Mage.

They realised that they were holding hands, and awkwardly took them back. A brief silence ensued.

"We've got a big job on, back home," said the Boffin.

"Yes, I want to do it though. Don't you?"

"Yes, but it gives me the shivers."

"That's possibly the wind through the window."

"Very funny," she said, laughing.

The first day they walked along the beach exploring. They found rock pools and caves, they found starfish and crabs. They found blue seaweed and purple seagrass. They found a large daisy like flower that grew between the rocks high above the waterline. Seagulls patrolled the sky and probed in the sand and the rock pools.

The second day they were holding hands. They walked around the point and in the distance they saw a huge twin peaked mountain on the horizon. The bay beyond the point swept round in the direction of the mountain, the blue swirled sands inviting them to walk as far as they could. They declined and turned back to their beach. They talked and talked. They swam, they just lazed around.

The third day they kissed. They had been for swim and the Boffin had put on a wrap-around skirt. They leaned on the bar at the edge of the veranda and looked out at the blue-green sea. They both started to say something and turned to look at each other. The Mage leaned in and kissed her.

She said, "Oh!" and turned away for a second.

Then she turned back and kissed him back.

"Do you think that Simon knew something?" she said between kisses.

"I don't know. Maybe. I don't care. Do you?"

"No. Of course not."

"Oh look! A humming bird."

The big climber that wreathed their cabin had come into flower and the small birds were hovering over them sipping nectar from the deep flowers.

"Oh they're lovely."

The fourth day they climbed the small hill behind the cabin. Half way up the hill they came across a clearing and rooting in the ground under a tree was a small pig. It was almost as surprised as they were and grunted and ran off away from them. They pressed on up the hill, and found that the top was a rocky outcrop, and scrambled up the last couple of metres. They sat on top of the outcrop and ate the sandwiches that they had dialled up on the 'oven'.

"This space of Simon's is beautiful, isn't it."

She squirmed around and laid her head in his lap. He stroked her hair.

"Yes," he said. "But we could do the same."

"Mmm, maybe. Or we could just explore others, like dragon space. That's beautiful in other ways."

She sat up. "What's that down there?"

"It looks like a temple or something, covered in vegetation. It's just behind the beach, about one hundred metres from the cabin, I'd say. Want to take a look?"

"Yeah. It should be safe. I don't think anything here will harm us. But tomorrow?"

They lazed around the top of the hill for a bit, then strolled back down to the beach. There was no sign of the piglet, except for a few patches where it had been rooting around under the trees. A few birds with fantastic tail feathers flitted between the trees.

They swam in the ocean, diving to pick up shells from the bottom and watched the multicoloured fish that swam around their legs unafraid. They walked on the beach and spotted a bush in the vegetation above the tide line with small round succulent fruits on it and ate their fill. The Mage dropped one of the fruits and a small furry hopping creature made a dash and claimed it in its small furry claws. It was so comical that they dropped a few more fruits, and others dashed out to retrieve the bounty.

On the fifth day they visited the temple. It wasn't a proper temple, they decided, but only a building built to look like a temple. They couldn't detect and Magic or Science in it, so they decided to enter it.

Inside it was bright, with tables and chairs, and what they decided to call the altar. The altar was covered in a lined cloth and had a lighted candlestick at each end. The Mage tried to lift one of them, but it was attached to a lever. As he pulled it the wall behind the altar rose into the roof, revealing a corridor behind it.

The Boffin ducked into the corridor and the Mage let go of the candlestick, only for the wall behind the altar to descend, cutting him off from the Boffin. He pulled on the candlestick and nothing happened. In a panic, he lifted the other candlestick, but it was just a candlestick.

He searched around for another lever or hidden switch. Nothing! Then the wall behind the altar rose once more.

"Come on," said Boffin. "I'm holding it open. It's a giant puzzle!"

He ducked through the entrance and hugged the Boffin.

"Worried were you?" she said laughingly.

"You don't know how much."

She kissed him. "I probably do. It took me a while to find the switch. Let's explore."

"Nothing is going to hurt us here in this space. I feel it," she said.

"Yes, I agree. It's designed for fun, so it's going to be safe."

"Interesting," she said. "I'm supposed to be the analytical one, but I was going by my feelings. You had a logical reason, and you are supposed to the dealer in beliefs and dreams."

"Maybe they aren't so far apart after all. Or maybe Simon's accident brought Science and Magic closer together."

They spent the rest of the day exploring the temple, from the depths of the dungeons, to the observatory on the roof. The Boffin excelled at the logic puzzles but the Mage was as good in his field of excellence. When there was no obvious route to follow, at an intersection of two corridors for example, the Mage led the way.

On the sixth day, their last full day, they strolled on the beach, past the temple, to a broad white and blue sandy river mouth. They let the water run over their feet and paddled their way across. On the other side was a colony of seal like

81

creatures with crests on their heads. Seagulls flew overhead raucously searching for titbits that the seals might drop.

"Phew, they stink!" said the Boffin.

"That's what a fish diet does for you, I suppose."

They strolled on for a while, watching the thin legged sea birds delving in the sand at the water's edge, and peering at small darting fish trapped in the rock pools. They carried on until they reached a deep flowing river much bigger than the one that they had crossed. Small reptiles dozed on the rocks as they absorbed the sunlight.

"Time to head back," said the Mage. The Boffin sighed and turned back. She matched steps and held his arm. He stopped and kissed her and they moved on.

After their meal that evening, they sat together in the swing chair on the veranda.

"I love you, dear Boffin," said the Mage.

"I love you, dear Mage. But? There was a 'but' there," she replied.

The Mage sighed. "Doesn't it seem awfully convenient to you? That we became Mage and Boffin, whatever that is, and fell in love in a couple of days?"

"Do you have any married friends? How did they meet?"

"Yes, one couple met at a bus stop when the bus was cancelled. And another couple met when they signed up for the same course."

"What if the bus had come on time? What if they'd decided on different courses?"

"Well they wouldn't have met, would they, and they wouldn't have.... Oh, I see."

"Any life event is unlikely, if you calculate the probabilities. Any event. If you prefer another way of saying it, they were destined to meet. We were destined to meet and fall in love. Everything else follows on from that. I don't know whether things are predestined, or whether we can choose our course in life. I don't care, if I have you. Another way of looking at it would be that we were chosen because we would fall in love."

"Wise woman. Will you marry me?"

She snuggled up to him. "Yes of course. I thought that you'd never ask."

On the morning of the seventh day they had just breakfasted and had a swim. They dressed in the clothes that they had arrived in, which had turned up in their clothes cupboards clean and neatly pressed.

"I could do with one of those cupboards," said the Boffin. "Imagine! No more washing or ironing."

The Mage laughed. "Yes, me too!"

They walked out onto the veranda.

"What now," the Mage wondered.

"Look, there's a boat," said the Boffin.

It didn't appear to have a motor but was headed directly for them. In the front stood Simon.

"That's not Simon, that's an automaton," said the Mage.

The boat rammed up on the shore and the automaton Simon strode up to them.

"Time's up," it said. "Time to go back."

The idyllic space faded and was replaced by the blasted landscape where they had met Simon, but there was no sign of anyone. They headed in the direction of the centre of the town, and there were a few people about. The Mage stopped a passer-by.

"Do you know where Simon is?"

"No idea. Do you mean the King? He's at the palace, I expect." He pointed down the road.

"Hey! I can understand you. What's happened? You must know. Why can't I understand anyone else?"

"What's your name, sir?" asked the Boffin.

"Zeb," said the passer-by. "Even my wife can't remember it. Come think of it, I can't remember hers." He looked bemused.

"Sorry, Zeb. We don't know what is going on either. Maybe the King will know."

Zeb nodded. "Good luck to you. I hope someone can sort this out."

The Mage and the Boffin headed down the hill. In places the recent conflicts had damaged buildings or the roadways. At the bottom, in the town centre was a large building, with a big sign outside that read "Town Hall".

People were about, mostly arguing frustratedly with each other. Or not. Most interactions seemed to end in frustration. The Mage and the Boffin headed for the doors which had a sign "Council Chamber" on them. A large man stepped up in front of them and folded his arms.

"You can't come in," he said.

"Why not?" asked the Boffin.

The large man reacted with shock. "You understand me!"

The Boffin looked at the Mage. "A pattern," she said.

"Yes, we understand you. Can we see Simon now?"

"Simon? You mean the King?" He seemed confused. "I guess so."

The Boffin and the Mage pushed through the doors, and into the room. Simon was sitting in the Mayor's chair, shouting at an elderly man.

"I don't care! Just find them for me."

The elderly man said "I don't understand you, sir."

"He doesn't understand you, Simon. Don't be angry with him," said the Boffin.

"Boffin! Mage! Where have you been?"

"Where you sent us, a week ago, Simon."

"I did? What's going on? Some guys rushed up and dragged me down here and put me in this throne. Why?"

"You don't remember? You got hit by some power, Magic and Science, that gave you huge power for a short time. You stopped the war and made us Mage and Boffin, and sent us off for a week to a paradise space. You gave us most of your power, and, it seems, you made it so that people can talk but no one can understand anyone else. Except us, apparently," said the Boffin.

The Boffin turned to the elderly man. "Can you please get us some tea, sir? I would love some."

The elderly man turned to go. "They understand me, and I understand them," he muttered and shuffled off.

"Simon, it seems that the little power you retained has made you King. This is actually the Town Hall and that is the Mayor's chair. We can help you become King, and I suggest that we start your reign here and make this town your capital."

Simon spread his hands. "I didn't want to be King, but something tells me I must be. I am in your hands."

The elderly man came back bearing a tray with the tea. "Can you tell him he's sitting in my chair?"

"Oh, sorry, Mr Mayor. That is King Simon's chair for now," said the Mage.

"Thank you for the tea, Mr Mayor," said the Boffin. "We'll get your chair back to you as soon as possible. Could you please leave us for a while?"

The Mayor said "Sure. You guys seem to know what's going on. No one ever tells me anything."

He shuffled off, muttering.

"Let's all join hands for a minute. We need as much power as we can get for this."

So the three of them joined hands.

"Can we fix up the language?" asked the Boffin.

"It doesn't seem so," said the Mage. "But we can create a new one."

"How can we distribute it? We can't do it person by person."

"Give it to me," said Simon. "Then when I talk to anyone they will understand, and they will be able to speak to me in the new tongue. They will then pass it on. When everyone speaks it, it will stop being special and become mundane. Children will then learn it naturally from their parents."

"Good idea. How long will it take, dear?" said the Boffin.

"Fifteen minutes if we all use our power."

The Mage laid out his charms and the Boffin linked them with her equations, and Simon added a few directions and suggestions. The language started from a word, became a sentence and grew into a paragraph, then a dictionary and a thesaurus, some dialects and a smidgen of slang and a few research papers and technical books of scientific words and a grimoire of magic and superstition. This became the core of the language.

The Mage added emotion and belief, the Boffin added logic and reason, while Simon added governance and direction, as well as freedom and latitude. Since it was going to be a real language they added a few negative elements, like bigotry, envy, and regretfully they allowed in grief and pain. They had to add those, even though they didn't want to do so.

The core of the language became a silver pearl in the Mage's hand. He gave it to Simon who swallowed it. The Mage gestured and the language expanded in Simon's brain.

"I think I've got it," Simon said. "Let's start sending it out there."

He went to the door and opened it. The security man turned towards him and Simon said "Let it be known that I, King Simon, require that all leading politicians and business leaders attend me here at their earliest convenience. You sir, what is your name?"

"Smith, sire, your Majesty," said the confused security man.

"You will be half of my personal security guard. You will need to get someone to take your place outside the door and you will need to appoint another security guard to be the other half of my personal security. Please go ahead and set that up."

"What about the language, sire? No one can understand anyone else."

"That has been resolved. Anyone you talk to will be able to understand you, and you will be able to understand them. OK?"

"Yes, sire. I'll get my friend Jones to be your other personal guard and I'll start getting that message out there."

Smith closed the door and the Mage and the Boffin and the new King returned to the table.

"My tea is cold," said the Boffin. With a gesture she heated it up again and took a satisfied sip.

"What little power I retained tells me that the world will be totally different from now onwards," said Simon. "There will be no Empire of Science and no Empire of Magic, though I can see that both magic and science will still battle for dominance, just not for total domination. And you, my friends, represent those two paradigms. Is there anything that I can do for you?"

"We will be busy helping you establish your kingdom for the next few years, sire. We will not have much free time, but we can't wait. We would like you to marry us today, sire, if you would be so kind," said the Mage.

The Boffin nodded. The new King asked them to hold hands, then he declared that they were man and wife, and added that this was a marriage of magic and science. This is why the custom is that all marriages are declared to be between those two paradigms.

Later, in their suite at the hotel that King Simon had arranged for them, they were cuddled up on the sofa. The Mage had his arm around her, and she was leaning against him, with her feet up on the sofa.

"We'll have to let our families know that we are married," said the Boffin. "They will be a bit annoyed that we've done it without them, but I didn't want to wait."

The Mage nodded. "But communications have been terrible because of the war. They'll understand."

Just then two ghostly figures appeared in front of them, gradually solidifying until they could see that they were an old man and woman.

"Pure science," said the Boffin looking at one of her instruments.

"And pure magic," said the Mage.

They looked at each other, puzzled.

"Ooof, mind if we sit down?" said the old man. "We're not as young as we used to be."

"Who are you?" asked the Mage. "How did you do that?"

"We're the Boffin and the Mage," said the old woman. "Or we were. You've taken over the mantle now. We just had to meet you before we go."

"You're our predecessors?"

"Yes, and we're ageing fast. We want to wish you luck. We have enjoyed our time in the roles."

"Yes, we've not regretted a minute of it," said the old man. "I don't think that you will either. We tried too hard at the start, but learned that you can't fix all the problems. Once we understood that, we managed a lot better."

"I like that solution for the language problem," said old lady. "Letting it spread like a virus was a good idea."

The old man and the old woman stood up and shook hands with their successors.

"Now we can briefly go back to our old names. What were they, my dear? I've forgotten," asked the old man.

"Adam and Eve, dear," said the old woman as they faded quietly away.

***

Ella and the Prince

Ella was like a normal seventeen-year old teenage girl, or boy for that matter. In other words, by turns gentle and aggressive, friendly and antagonistic, loving and hating, helpful and obstructive, kind and spiteful. The hormonal storms of puberty had mostly died down, but still flared up now and then.

It hadn't helped that her mother had died when she was seven, and that her father had married a divorced woman with two sons when Ella was in the middle of changing from a child to a woman. In general Ella and her step-Mum got on well, as Ella could see that her Dad was happy again, and her new step brothers, one of whom was usually at University, weren't too unbearable, she thought.

When Ella was in a good mood, she called her step-mother 'Mum'. When she wasn't, what she called her would best be left untold. Her step-mother tried to ignore the worst of the storms.

From the description above, you might think that she was a brat, but that is far from the case. Mostly her home life was tranquil and contented, with only a few blow ups to disturb the family calm. Ella was well aware of what was going on in her body, and when she did have a flare up, she would let it die down, and then apologize and be especially nice to her step-mother for a while. Then her step-mother would talk about the problems that she'd had when her sons were going through similar hormonal storms. They would usually end up laughing hysterically.

Her step-mother on her part, loved Ella to bits. She had not been lucky enough to have a girl baby in her previous marriage, but she came from a family of girls and understood what Ella was going through and made allowances. Ella did love her step-mother, but with a bit of reserve. She sometimes felt that she was betraying her mother by loving her step-mother so much. Over time though, it seemed more and more right.

One thing, though, was almost guaranteed to cause a big fight and that was housework. Ella had a blind-spot and if she was asked to vacuum the house or dust around, or iron clothes, the chances were that she would spin up into a rage. She considered that she did more of the housework than both of the boys combined. Well, she might have had a point, if it was true that the boys didn't ever do those jobs, but in fact, they did. But they also did the washing up or put the dishes into the machine, cleaned the shower and the toilet, cut the grass, took out the garbage and even washed the car now and then, none of which Ella was asked to do. Somehow this didn't help.

But if Ella was asked to do housework, she would explode, then she would sulk, and then she would apologize to her step-mother, then she would do it. It worried her a little that such a tiny thing could cause her such grief.

"Don't worry, dear. You'll grow out of these moods," said her step-mother, hoping that she was right.

Ella would give her a hug and do the chore, whatever it was.

It so happened that Ella and her family lived not far from the Royal Summer Palace. The Royal family spent a month or so at the Summer Palace most years and the locals eagerly awaited the visits, because the local economy was boosted by the spending of the Royals and the media and others who followed them around.

There were also the parties! The Royals tended to hold gala balls and banquets but the Crown Prince held parties! Famous classical musicians were hired for the balls and banquets, but famous pop groups were hired for the Prince's parties.

Of course, you couldn't just turn up for one of the Prince's parties. There was a ballot held and on the occasion that we are interested in, all three step-siblings won a ticket. Great rejoicing! It happened that Ella's father and step-mother were going to visit some friends on the same evening and would be out too.

On the day, all the family were preparing to leave for the evening. Ella wore her favourite LBD and paired it with heeled shoes. She had her hair trimmed and swept to one side. As it was a masque party, she had a black domino mask with sequinned edges. She looked amazing.

Unfortunately she had forgotten to do one of the chores that her step-mother had asked her to do.

"Right, please get changed and sweep the floors in here and in the kitchen and vacuum the lounge. I've asked you several times, and I told you that you weren't going out until you had done it," said her step-mother.

Ella immediately had a meltdown. She screamed and shrieked and begged, but to no avail. Even her father wouldn't help her.

"Go and get changed. You are not going out tonight until it is done, and that's final," said her step-mother firmly.

Ella flew up to her bedroom and fell on her bed crying. She was going to miss the party! After a bit she calmed down and changed to her ordinary clothes, and started to do the chores. Stupid temper! She resolved to never to have a meltdown again. She conveniently ignored the fact that she'd promised herself the same thing several times before.

It didn't take her long to finish the chores and the repetitive motions were soothing. She finished and sat down. What now?

"I can still go!" she told herself. It wasn't too late! She looked at herself in the mirror. OK, she looked like a panda, but she could fix that! She quickly washed off her make-up, and reapplied it. OK, it wasn't as good as it was before, but it would do. She slipped on her LBD and her shoes. Mmm, the hair was a mess. She did her best, and the end result was still amazing. She donned the mask, and picked up her black clutch and was ready to go.

As a last touch she put on a necklace that she had been given by her mother, which had a gold chain and a green polished stone teardrop pendant. She carefully locked up the house and headed for the Summer Palace. From some distance she could make out the thumping sound of the music and as she got closer she could even make out the song that was playing. Looking forward to the party, she mounted the steps to the door.

"Excuse me, miss, can I please see your ticket?" asked one of the large men at the door.

She dipped in her clutch and then realised. Oh no, she'd left it on the table!

"I can't let you in without a ticket," stated the large man.

"I've got a ticket, but I left it at home."

The large man just shook his head. She refused to cry. She walked away from the door with her head down. She WASN'T going to CRY.

"Think she was genuine, Smith?" asked the other large man.

"Probably, Jones," said the other. "But you know the rules."

Ella walked down the road to the corner, then turned right. This was not the way home, of course. She circled the building. Ah, an open window! She considered. A bin! Right. She pushed the bin under the window. Somehow she scrambled up on to the bin. After a bit of thought she slipped off her shoes and held them in her mouth by the straps. Yuk! Awful taste.

She pulled the window open and pushed herself through head first, into what looked like a storeroom. At first, she was able to control her descent but suddenly she was shooting through the air. Crash! She hit the floor with a bang.

"Ooof!" she said. She slipped her shoes on just as two pages rushed in to see what was happening.

"Come on, dear, you're out."

They pulled her through the door into the room where the party was happening. They hurried her towards the exit, but suddenly a voice called out, "Wait! What's happening here?"

"We have caught someone who was trying to get in without a ticket, sire," said one of the pages.

"I've got a ticket! I just left it at home."

Everyone laughed. Ella realised that the party had come to a stop.

"Come here, my dear," said the Prince.

The pages brought her before the Prince.

"Pretty little thing," said the Prince. "Well, am I worth it?"

He threw his arms up, and a few people sniggered.

"****!" she said quietly, so that only he could hear.

The Prince laughed, and she ran for the exit, in her heels, bumping into people on the way. She burst out of the door and flew down the steps.

The two large men watched her go.

"You left the window open, Smith."

"So it appears, Jones."

"She didn't make proper use of the opportunity."

"Poor girl. I'd better go and shut it. One's enough for a night."

Ella headed home, crying, expressing her opinion of the Prince and her life as she went. She stepped off the kerb and one of her heels broke off.

"Should've gone back and got the dratted ticket! Should've gone back and got the dratted ticket!"

She stopped and removed both shoes and carried them in her hand. A truck went past and the driver leant on his horn. She made a gesture at him.

She arrived home and went to her room and removed all her make-up, then changed into her pyjamas and went down and watched television.

After a while her Dad and step-Mum arrived home from their friends' house.

"Quiet evening?" said her Dad.

"You might say that," she answered, not exactly truthfully. "I think I'll wait up for the boys."

"OK, dear," said her step-mother. "We're going to bed."

She leapt up and hugged her step-mother. "I l-l-love you," she said.

Her step-mother patted her on the back. She looked over Ella's head at Ella's Dad questioningly. Ella's Dad indicated that he had no idea.

Ella settled down to watch the television, although she didn't see much of what appeared on the screen. Shortly after Council Noise Control shut down the party at one in the morning her step-brothers came home.

They walked in chatting and saw her waiting for them.

"Oh, the star turn," said Matt, the older brother.

She wailed. "Really?"

"Sorry, Ella. Yes, everyone was talking, but don't worry. Your mask was in place and no one, except us, guessed. Everyone was wondering who you were. We were the only ones to guess because we know you so well, and we weren't telling."

"Oh, thanks guys! I love you both!"

"Someone might work it out, though. There were a lot of people there that know you. Let's hope that they don't."

"Who would have thought that the Prince was such a ....."

"****?" offered Robin. "Yes, it was pretty nasty."

"Oh no!" she said. "I've lost my mother's necklace."

"Go to bed, kid, it will be better in the morning. Maybe someone will hand it in. We'll ask."

Nevertheless, she spent a restless night. In the morning, another blow. The news was full of a story about a mystery interloper who had crashed the Prince's party. The interloper had been ejected, according to the inaccurate story, before she managed to approach the Prince. A fuzzy picture was shown. Ella cringed.

Then a shock. Her necklace was shown, together with a number to call. Robin and Matt looked at her. Ella realised that there was no way out.

"Er, Dad? Can I tell you something?"

The whole sorry story came out. Her Dad and her step-mother looked at each other.

"You can call, or not," her Dad said.

"I'll call," she said.

She called the number and was given an appointment.

"Can you come with me, Mum? Please?" she asked her step-mother.

They turned up at the Summer Palace and were directed to a waiting room. It was partly panelled with walnut, and the doors and furniture were walnut. The top part of the walls was painted in an eggshell blue, and the ceiling ornaments were white. The lights and the fans were brass. There were portraits on the walls, and a very big painting of a large house. They had a long time to notice the details. Someone brought them some tea and biscuits.

Eventually the Crown Prince arrived, accompanied by a young Army officer, his brother. He sat down at the table with them.

"Hullo, sorry for the wait. It's nice to meet you again. I'm very sorry for the way I behaved last night. I should not have made fun of you in front of everyone. You were correct when you called me that name. What's your name, by the way?"

Ella swallowed. "Erm, I'm Ella. Do you have my necklace, sire? It was my Mum's."

The Crown Prince glanced at Ella's step-mother.

"Step-mother," Ella's step-mother explained.

"Well, Ella, when you made your escape, you bumped into my brother, and your necklace caught on his uniform. Yes, he has your necklace."

The young officer said "Hullo, Ella, I'm Mark. Unfortunately the chain snapped when your necklace caught on my uniform."

He placed it on the table.

"If you permit me, I'll get it mended before I return it to you. I want to."

"Thank you. I'd like that."

The Crown Prince said "You might like to know that I was severely told off by our parents for the way I treated you. And by Mark. And by pretty much everyone else who knows me. I realised pretty much right away that I had been a... what you called me. I sincerely apologise to you."

"Thank you, sire," said Ella. "I'm sorry I caused such a commotion. If only I'd remembered my ticket."

They chatted for a short time, until the Princes had to leave. Ella found the Crown Prince to be charming, in spite of their unfortunate first meeting, but she liked the younger Prince better. She wondered without any real expectation if he would ask her out when he returned the necklace, and she couldn't know that Prince Mark was planning to do exactly that. The future is unknown, but in at least one possible future, she was going to attend the Crown Prince's wedding by the side of her husband, Prince Mark. Let's hope that future came to pass.

***

The Boy Who Followed the Dragons

Now and then someone spotted a dragon. It was usually flying high in the sky, but no one knew where it was going to or why. Occasionally a dragon could be seen perched on a peak, resting or attending to its wings, or feeding on a cow that it had taken.

Sometimes a sighting of a dragon would be considered good luck, and sometimes it would be considered bad luck. Not that it made any difference in the end.

Patrick, or Paddy to those few friends he had, was obsessed with dragons. He read all the dragon fan magazines and watched all the films that contained dragons. He corresponded with other dragon fanciers but was often disappointed by their lack of knowledge.

"Dragons do not have four legs!" he wrote to one fan magazine. "If they had four legs and two wings, that would give them six limbs, since wings are modified limbs. They are not insects! They have two wings and two legs. Four limbs."

Nevertheless, people kept drawing dragons with four legs and two wings and it infuriated him. But no one had ever photographed a dragon, at least in enough detail to show the number of legs. Eye witnesses without cameras described, in Paddy's opinion, beasts which couldn't possibly exist. Three eyes or more. Crests like antlers. Glowing eyes, and breath of fire.

He considered the reports and divided them into categories. He set aside those which to him seemed fantastic, but he didn't reject them totally.

Then there were those that were made by farmers and shepherds, who described how sheep and cows were taken by dragons. In general, they described the dragons as descending on bat like wings, and snatching and carrying off cattle in their jaws.

There were the reports of dragons perching on peaks, and these almost all described the dragon in an upright posture, like a bird. There were reports from pilots who had seen them from the air, and they described them as bird-like or bat-like.

Then there were the Kings. The Kings (and some Queens) retreated to The Castle, and reportedly changed into dragons, which then flew off. Paddy was troubled by this. If Kings had been changing into dragons for as long as recorded history, then dragons should be as common as sparrows, he thought. But they were rare.

It didn't fit, but he had to accept it as fact. There were even blurry photographs. The only alternative was that the Crown had been faking the transformations for centuries, and that was not possible or credible. However, the descriptions did fit with Paddy's opinion that dragons had four limbs, comprised of two legs and two wings.

Paddy's room was covered in posters of dragons, news articles about dragons and various drawings of dragons. He had books about dragons, magazines about dragons. He wrote articles for the dragon magazines, theorising all sorts of things about them.

For his articles, he wondered about their diet, how they reproduced, and what they were doing when they were seen flying through the skies. He knew that they ate meat, since the occasional cow was reportedly stolen by a dragon, but he was unsure if they also ate vegetable matter. He assumed as did most people who were interested in dragons, that they laid eggs, as many reptiles do. Paddy didn't consider them to be reptiles, but to be a related class of creature. In this belief he was in a minority, and this often caused heated discussions in the dragon fan magazines. He was also wrong. Dragons are a class of reptile.

Two things puzzled him about dragons. The first was the relationship with humans if any. There was the King thing, of course, but folk-tales were full of heroes slaying dragons. In most cases the question was, why? Often the dragon was supposed to be devastating the area by killing cattle, it is true, but in the modern era such dragons as took a cow or a sheep always moved on. Sometimes the storybook dragons amassed great amounts of jewellery and precious items. Paddy thought it unlikely, as what use were jewels to a dragon? So the question remained : why were humans so obsessed by dragons? Why were folk-tales full of them?

The second was how they managed to fly. A dragon would be a heavy beast, about the same weight as a man. Dragon wings would have to be huge to support their weight and the bones that formed the structure of the wings would have to be thick and solid, but that would make it impossible for the dragon to fold them, and the muscles necessary to drive the wings would be immense.

So Paddy became something of an expert on dragons, even though he had never seen one. He searched all the scientific literature and the magical tomes for information about dragons, made deductions, compared this document with that grimoire, and in the end, found that people asked him about dragons rather than the other way round.

It was a great surprise and a shock to his father and mother when Paddy disappeared. He'd announced to them that he was "going to check out something out about dragons," and that he would be back in a couple of weeks. Since he was twenty-three, and had done this once or twice before, his parents weren't concerned, but when he had been away for a month, they started to get worried.

They employed a private investigator to try to find him. The PI found that he had travelled south to a provincial town, and then told locals that he was going on a hike to the south-west and no one had seen him since. The PI eventually found his camp, but he hadn't been there for a long time, so the PI returned Paddy's camping gear to his parents.

They employed a magical investigator next, but when he was given some of Paddy's clothes to touch he was confused and surprised.

"Are you sure that these are his clothes? Are they perhaps new and unworn? Second hand?" he asked.

"No, those are Paddy's clothes. He's definitely worn them, " answered his father.

"That's strange. I can't detect him anywhere. Where did you say he was seen last?"

Paddy's father told him. The MI went to the area to check it out.

"I can see traces of whoever wore these clothes down there," he reported, "but then nothing."

"Is he dead?"

"No, I would have found traces of him, his aura would still be around for years. No one can just vanish. Except it seems, your son."

Paddy's parents hoped against hope that Paddy would suddenly return, but as time went on that hope faded. Then all of a sudden one day, after about a year, Paddy came back.

The phone rang one day, and Paddy's mother answered it.

"This is the police. We have found your son. He's in a bit of a state. Disoriented. But he's safe."

"Oh thank, thank you. Where is he? Can we see him?"

The constable on the phone told them that he was at a place many kilometres from home and far from the place where he had disappeared.

"We'll send him home, but he will have to go to the hospital there. He's got a bad cut on his cheek, and a couple on his body. Oldish wounds, but not disfiguring. He says that he was fighting for the Queen, and goes on about flying and dragons and stuff. I think he's in shock."

Eventually Paddy returned home to them. He'd have a scar on his face for life, but it wasn't too noticeable. He decided to grow a beard and cover it. He went up to his room and looked at all his dragon posters, his notebooks, and magazines. He sighed and started to clear them out.

"I don't need them any more. It's mostly rubbish any way," he explained, and cut all ties with the dragon enthusiast communities.

So what caused this change of heart? This is what happened to Paddy when he followed the dragons.

***

Paddy was poring over some appearance statistics, plotting them on a map using his computer. He wondered what they would look like in three dimensions on a globe. He was stunned to find that they fell in groups on circles around the globe, and that all the circles met at two points on either side of the globe. One point fell in the middle of the ocean, but the other fell on land, way down in the Southern Provinces. He called them the Dragon Poles.

He looked in the literature and found that he wasn't the first person to spot the pattern, but the dry scientific paper he read didn't make much of it.

He had to go and have a look. He HAD to. He sold one of his pieces of dragon memorabilia and bought a plane flight to the nearest centre. He told his parents, kissed them, then set off. Fortunately he was able to take time off from his job. Little did he know that he wouldn't be back for some time.

On the flight down he naturally scanned the skies for dragons and naturally, he didn't see any. He hired a car and drove as near as he could to the Dragon Pole.

"What are your plans, sir?" asked the landlady at the bed and breakfast place that he stayed at.

"Oh, I'm going to do some hiking south-west of here," he said.

"You'll love it," said the landlady. "It's beautiful out there."

"Can I leave my car and bags here?" Paddy asked. "I'm just taking my camping gear."

"Sure dear," said the landlady. This would be one of the last traces of Paddy that the PI would find.

Paddy set off into the wilderness. He had some maps of the area and was used to camping. It took him three days to reach the area that contained his Dragon Pole, and he set up camp there to consider his next steps. He had brought along a detector which should indicate if dragons were near and a charm which should do the same thing.

He switched on the detector and immediately it indicated dragons in the neighbourhood. Unfortunately it didn't indicate the direction, and a quick look around showed no visible dragons. He activated the charm. This time the charm indicated that yes, there were dragons nearby, and at the same time, that they were far away. Hmm, confusing.

He cooked himself a meal and pondered. Dragons around and both near and far. What on earth did that mean? He puzzled over it as he ate the meal, and hadn't come to any conclusions by the time he was preparing for bed. He damped his fire down and darkness closed in.

Something crossed in front of the moon. But it was too quick. Was it a dragon, or merely an owl or night flying bird? Somewhat grumpily he settled down for the night.

The next morning, after his breakfast he moodily looked his two instruments. The scientific one still showed dragons all around. He tried shielding the antenna with some foil to get a direction but it didn't work.

The magical instrument wasn't much better. It indicated dragons close and dragons distant. He suddenly realised that it was showing a direction! But it wasn't the usual north, south, east, or west direction. It was something else.

Without thinking, he took a step in that direction. Suddenly he was on the top of a crag which jutted out into an incredible valley, deep and forbidding, still shadowed by the surrounding peaks which would keep sun light out until the sun was high in the sky.

And the rising sun! It had a halo around it and the halo was pink. Paddy looked at it for a moment and spun around. He tried to step back, but stayed on the crag where he had arrived.

A little shocked, he looked around. He realised that he was stuck here, in this **other space**. Franticly he stepped backwards and forwards, but he didn't go anywhere.

"Oh no!" he said to himself.

He sat down on the crag and thought about his plight. He remembered that he'd been trying to find dragons when he had stepped into this space. He looked around and there they were! Not far away, and rising and falling, hovering on an updraft, and he could hear them calling to one another. They swirled in a spiral, then settled onto the rocks.

He bugled a call to them (bugled?) and saw them turn towards him. He dropped into the valley, and caught an updraft with his wings (wings?), and soared over to join them. He back-pedalled with his wings and dropped down onto a spare rock between them, his claws scraping on the rock (claws?). The other dragons made space for him but one or two rumbled at him. One small female dragon kept snapping at his feet until he hissed at her.

It's fair to say that the dragon that Paddy had become wasn't too worried about having left the human space. In fact the essential part that was Paddy shrank and was compressed into a small pearl that sat in a space just above the dragon brain. The pearl didn't sever all ties to the dragon brain that was originally a small part of Paddy's brain, and was now the major part, but it was only tenuously attached.

Paddy, as I will call the dragon that was once Paddy the human, was not immediately accepted by the rest of the dragons. A few of the older ones grumbled and muttered at him, and the less mature kept challenging him. But then, they challenged each other all the time too. The females, all small and immature, were openly hostile to him at first, hissing and pecking at him. Dragons don't usually form groups, but Paddy had stumbled into their space at a special time.

Gradually he fitted in. Dragons only formed loose groups at these special times, which often split and reformed, so the group was used to welcoming newcomers. As they swept down the long deep valleys, to the open plains beyond to hunt, they bonded by doing acrobatic flight tricks, swooping mere millimetres from rock faces and diving through narrow gaps and holes in the rock. Shrieking, the whole group would play follow my leader through the chasms and ledges that abounded in this space.

For the gravity was weaker here, and water ran slower down hill, tumbling in seeming slow motion from rocky cliffs to deep pools, fountaining up when the slow moving streams met boulders in the river beds. And gravity did not pull so hard on the mountains, which meant that the mountains were higher and steeper than in the human space.

Out on the plains the dragons hunted the roving food beasts who ran endlessly from horizon to horizon for their whole lives. When the dragons appeared so did a flock of smaller dragons with massive muscular jaws, and ground running reptiles with similar jaws. The scavengers.

The part of Paddy that was still human would have realised that he was accepted into the group when a small female and another male similar in size to Paddy joined with him in a hunt. The small female harassed and slowed the target beast and the male turned it towards Paddy. Paddy dropped onto it and broke its neck with a single bite.

The other two dragons joined him in devouring the dead food beast. They pulled the limbs from it, stripping the sweet meat from the bones and leaving the bones themselves to the scavengers, who hung around and darted in now and then to grab a morsel or two. The dragons ripped open the body and feasted on the nutrient rich entrails, the lungs, the liver, the heart and other tasty bits. As they filled their stomachs they ate slower and slower and the scavengers became bolder and the dragons only occasionally bothered to swat them away.

Finally, they finished eating and almost together they spread their wings to catch the breeze and with a couple of flaps rose into the air. They circled upwards barely clearing the air borne rush of the winged scavengers diving in to finish off the beast. Squabbles broke out between scavengers as they fought over the remains.

On the way back to the roost the dragons stopped off to eat the foliage of some bushes, probably for some nutrient that they could not get from the food beasts. Back at the roost, they picked a convenient rock to perch on and while they didn't sleep as such, they shut down many of their bodily processes, and went comatose. Small parasitic reptiles trying to suck their blood caused them to grumble and stir and shake during the night. Paddy caught one and chewed it ruminatively.

One morning instead of flying out to the plains the group flew down to one of the pools beneath one of this space's slow falling waterfalls. They dipped and splashed and played in the water for a while, then flew up and headed along the mountain range. Paddy the dragon was aware that dragons usually lived solitary lives, though they could often see their neighbours. Paddy the human, what there was left of him, wondered why they were congregating and where they were going.

They became aware of other groups also headed in the same direction, all breaking off their trips to chase down the food beasts once or twice a day, making the food beasts skittish and wary. Sometimes they had to travel quite a distance into the plains to find undisturbed food beasts.

A mountain came into view and Paddy the dragon knew that it was their destination. It had a tall spire of rock at the summit, much higher than would be possible on earth and the foot of the spire seemed to be surrounded by mist. As Paddy's group got closer, the mist resolved into a cloud of dragons, all milling around the ledge at the base of the spire.

The group drew closer and the dragons could be seen to be congregating in dozens of places. At the centres of the clouds were mature female dragons. They were not happy, snapping at their surrounding clouds of eager males. Immature females were being shoved aside in the melees and took up perches on ledges part way up the spire.

Mature female dragons, larger than the males, started to take off surrounded by many males. Some males dropped away and others rushed to catch up. One or two of Paddy's group of males left to join the fray, while the immature females in their group were pushed aside and took up station up on the spire with the other young females.

Paddy lost track of his group as it splintered, his former companions chasing different females. He scouted around some of the females and got pushed aside by other males. Another female took off taking another crowd of males. All was confusion, with males flying up and down, changing their minds from minute to minute.

Paddy was dragged up a few times, but circled back down again. The sky was full of female dragons each with their horde of males, and it would seem from a distance as if puffs of smoke were being emitted by the base of the spire.

Chaos still reigned but the press was reducing, with fewer females furiously fighting off the males, before taking flight. New females were coming out of the tunnel at the bottom of the spire, larger than the other females and several shades lighter. Paddy's dragon mind said "Queens", though dragon

Queens were not solitary rulers, like ant or bee queens. They were just long-lived mature females with vast experience.

Each Queen carried off her cloud of suitors, and the remaining males milled around waiting. Finally, the largest female yet came out of the tunnel. She was almost pure white and her weight was at least half as much again as Paddy's. Paddy's dragon mind said "**The** Queen".

The Queen flapped her enormous wings and took off with around three hundred males following her, including Paddy. There were still around a thousand or so males left behind, either because they were sick, or they had missed their chance to take part in the contest this time.

Paddy flew up with The Queen and her escort, avoiding the males who were injured in the melee and were descending to the ledge or who didn't have the energy to continue and who fell away. He used any thermal lift that he could find and screamed with joy as he picked one that few others did and rose up near to front of the chasing pack.

There was a group of about a dozen males who were cooperating in keeping the rest at arms length. Paddy bullied his way into the group, sustaining a few scratches in the process and displacing another exhausted male.

Paddy and his fellows steadily rebuffed the other males and eventually they all dropped away. Still they rose, until The Queen's rise slowed to a stop. One of the largest males darted in and grabbed The Queen, and they tumbled through the air, mating as they fell. The other males followed their fall.

The successful male let The Queen go, and she rose through the air again and the successful male spiralled down back to the spire from which they had started. Then The Queen's rise slowed again and Paddy tried to move in. He was beaten to it by another male. One of the other males dropped away exhausted at the same time, and the remaining males again followed The Queen and her latest suitor down as they tumbled and then flew up again.

Again Paddy tried to move in but was pushed aside by another male. He was slashed across the face for his trouble. The Queen and the new male tumbled away, and the group followed. The new male then dropped away and so did two of the remaining suitors.

By this time, Paddy was nearly exhausted. They all rose again and this time Paddy timed it right, and clasped The Queen, and they tumbled as they mated, while Paddy trumpeted his triumph. Then he let go of The Queen and tumbled exhaustedly for several hundred metres before he could halt his fall. He circled tiredly down to the spire and found a perch fairly close to the tunnel beneath the spire, nearly missing the landing from exhaustion.

Not long after Paddy landed, The Queen landed, snapping at the few remaining suitors who still followed her. She retired up her tunnel and all went quiet. Many of the males and most of the females had left. A few of the other Queens still clung to ledges on the sides of the spire, tired after their flights.

Paddy looked at the sun and saw that it was starting to descend. He flew off back along the mountain range and drank at a waterfall. He stopped at a mountain meadow and tore up vegetation displacing the small animals living in it. He then headed out onto the plains. He spotted some commotion down on the ground and dropped down to see what was going on. Yes! The remains of a food beast were being squabbled over by scavengers. He chased them off and ate as much as he could tear off, but there wasn't much left on the carcass. He

111

cracked a few bones for the marrow, then tiredly flew back to the mountains to roost.

In the morning he had some luck when he was able to join up with a small group heading the same way as him. He and two other tired dragons managed to bring down a food beast. It wasn't a clean kill and something in him disliked that intensely, but the meat was sweet and the blood was warm, and he began to feel better.

He stuck with the group for a while, and then the group started to break up. He headed into the mountains and found a peak that looked good. He trumpeted to see who was around, and got replies from a few places around him. It would do. Not too close to others, not too isolated.

He rested for the next night, the next day, and the next night. When day next came he was about to call and head down to the plains when two humans appeared on his peak. He snorted in surprise and annoyance.

"He's nearly forgotten that he is a human," said the female. "His last human traces would have disappeared in a few months. We were just in time."

"I'll sort it," said the male, and made a gesture.

Paddy was a human again.

"What? Ah!" he said staggering.

"We've been looking for you. We had to come back in time, and it's very exhausting," said the female, grumpily.

"Don't be hard on him, my dear," said the male. "It's not his fault."

"Ah," said Paddy, trying to remember how to talk. "I came here and I couldn't get back. I followed the dragons. Who are you?"

"I'm the Boffin, and he's the Mage."

112

The names didn't mean anything to him.

"I mated with The Queen," he said.

"Yes, dear, we know. That's why we are here. The Queen will lay an egg and that egg will contain your offspring. The trouble is, that offspring will be human, a little girl. In the future, we rescued her and took her back to human space. The dragons asked us to. But we had to come back for you, just in case it happened again."

"Why did... Why didn't you just go back to when I stepped over and bring me back then? Why did you let me stay here for so long?"

"Your little girl. She would have been wiped from existence if we had done that. We couldn't do it. We'll take you back with us, but it will be hard for you. You will be confused for a while, as you've been a dragon for so long. In human space it's been a year, but here, it's been a couple of weeks. Don't talk about it too much or people will think you are crazy. You will keep your wounds, and will have scars, but they are not disfiguring. OK?"

"What are the Dragon Poles? I never did find out."

"Oh, they are the points in the two spaces that are always in sync on the dragon planet and the human planet. Think of the surfaces of the two planets as two concentric glass spheres and an axis running through the two spheres at the dragon poles. All points except the two poles can move in circles around one of the two poles, but it's like the poles are locked together."

Paddy thought about that, then shrugged. "I sort of see that, but why do the dragons move on great circles passing through those poles when they are in human space?"

The Mage looked at the Boffin.

"We don't know. We think that it is a 'shortcut' of some sort. The dragons only go to human space when they are travelling. That's a very good question."

She continued, "You know, you didn't need to travel to the Dragon Pole to step across. You could have done it anywhere. The key was to do it without thinking. That's why you found that you couldn't step back."

"But you are here to take me back."

Paddy looked around. In a human sort of way, he'd enjoyed his time here. In the dragon way, which was fading from his mind, he'd been a good dragon. Dragons felt joy over a clean kill, a swooping twisting flight through the canyons and valleys, and a successful mating. Oh and a good splash and shower under a slow falling waterfall.

"Let's go before I beg you to let me stay," he said.

The Mage and the Boffin held his hands.

"Step forward."

He did so, and found himself on a high moor, not far from a small town. He staggered under the unaccustomed gravity. He felt an urge to spread his wings. But he didn't have any.

"We've made it so that you will not jump off of things for a while, in case you try to fly. Try not to talk too much about being a dragon. We can't stop you doing that. You will be confused for a while, and we've tried to help you with that. We'll let you go and make yourself known to the constable in the village, now. If it is any consolation, things will turn out just fine."

"Do I get to see my daughter?"

The Boffin looked at the Mage.

"Yes, we will be in touch. We've given her to a Queen to adopt."

"Good," said Paddy. "She is the daughter of a Queen, after all, and I don't think that I'd be a good parent at the moment. Dragons don't look after their offspring for long. The males are often not involved at all."

Ten years later, the Mage and the Boffin appeared in Paddy's apartment. He'd had received a note that they were going to "drop in".

"Wow, when you say 'drop in' you really mean it," he joked.

"How are you, Paddy?" asked the Boffin, though they actually knew, because they had followed his career.

"Fine, though I suspect you know," said Paddy. "I should be elected mayor next year, and my wife is expecting our second baby in the spring. No wings expected," he joked.

"Can you come with us, for a few hours?" asked the Mage. "We'd like to introduce you to your daughter from the time when you were a dragon."

"Sure. My wife is at her mother's for the weekend, with our daughter, so that I would be free to go with you."

The Mage, the Boffin and Paddy held hands, and then they were outside a castle.

"Are the King and Queen expecting us?" asked Paddy. "Have you told them about, you know, how their daughter came about. They know that I am happy about them adopting her?"

"Yes, don't worry, it's all arranged."

They walked through the gates of the castle without being challenged, and a page showed them into a pleasant sitting room. King Edmund and Queen Charlotte were waiting. Also in the room was a small girl.

"May I present Princess Patricia, sometimes called Princess Paddy," said the Mage.

"Hullo, ma'am," said Paddy to Princess Paddy.

"Hullo, Paddy," said the Princess. "Are you really my daddy?"

Paddy looked at King Edmund and Queen Charlotte, and they nodded.

"Yes, ma'am, I am."

They shook hands, and as they touched something passed between them. Paddy and the Princess saw the landscape of the dragon space. In the foreground a dragon stretched and flapped his wings.

"Oh," said the Princess, "that's pretty. I'd like to go there."

The others in the room looked bemused.

"We got a glimpse of dragon space," explained Paddy.

Paddy stayed for most of the afternoon, talking to the Princess, about being a Princess, dragons, and all sorts of other things. Finally, it was time to go.

"You know I have to go, Pat," said Paddy. You couldn't have two Paddys, and they had settled on that.

"Yes, Paddy. But can you come back and visit, please?" the Princess asked.

"Of course. I'd love too. Goodbye for now, my dear."

He hugged the little Princess and left with the Mage and the Boffin.

"OK?" asked the Boffin.

"Yes, very OK, thanks. She's lovely, isn't she?"

When the Princess was older, with the permission of her adopted parents, and the approval of the Mage and the Boffin, Paddy took the Princess to the dragon space, "on holiday" as they called it, and they, as dragons, flew the valleys and canyons, hunted, killed and ate the food beasts, ripped up huge mouthfuls of tasty bushes, and splashed in the waterfalls and the pools beneath them. Dragons are solitary creatures, but they were much closer than normal dragons.

The Princess eventually married a local boy and invited Paddy to the wedding. The King gave the Princess away, but only because Paddy deferred to him. The King had wanted him to do the task. At the reception afterwards the Princess drew Paddy aside for a minute.

"Paddy, my dear father, our trips are over."

"I know, my dear Pat. I know. It's been fun."

"Oh yes! But I will get back there eventually, so the Boffin and the Mage tell me."

Paddy knew what that meant and didn't reply. He remained a friend of the Princess, and was close to her throughout her life. He was "sponsor father" of her children. We would say "god father". He was at her eldest daughter's wedding, although he was frail by then. When he died, the Princess was a mourner at his funeral.

She was over sixty when she started to eat voraciously and rapidly gained weight and slept a lot. She knew what it meant. She called the Mage and the Boffin, and they supported her and her family as much as they could. They transported her to a high tower and stood guard as she transitioned to a dragon. They watched as the new dragon flew into the heights and bugled. She got a response and followed it, stepping through to dragon space as a new immature female with a whole new life in front of her.

"That's a happy ending," said the Boffin.

The Mage nodded. "Yes, a satisfactory resolution, my dear. I checked her children and as far as I could tell, they are unlikely to pass over when they get older. This was a one off. Shall we go home?"

The Boffin kissed him. "Yes, dear, but we must visit dragon space again soon. It's so beautiful."

***

The Robot Life

The Boffin and the Mage were visiting the local market when they came across a tent with a sign outside it.

"'I say that I am a robot. Prove that I am really a person and win five dollars. Two dollars a try'," read the Mage. "Interesting. Shall we have a look?"

They entered the tent and sitting in front of them was what appeared to be a glum looking young man. He was slouched in a folding chair, holding a bloody cloth to his head.

"What happened here?" said the Boffin. She scanned him with one of her instruments.

"Oh, a guy came in here and tried to convince me with his fists. It's an approach that I hadn't anticipated, I must admit. He took the only two dollars that I'd made so far and wanted more." He sighed.

The Mage put four dollars down on the table, and he and the Boffin sat down.

"I think that I know how this is going to go," said the Mage. He looked at the Boffin. Logic and reason were nominally her territory, but neither of them was too worried about such matters.

"Magic is science that hasn't been explained," the Boffin used to say.

"And science is magic that has been explained," the Mage would respond.

"But how do we know that the explanation is correct?" the Boffin followed up.

"Only time will tell," concluded the Mage.

He looked at the robot. "You are a robot. You are programmed to respond exactly as a person would respond in any given situation. For example, you may appear to feel pain, but you do not, because as a robot, you are not conscious, and therefore cannot feel anything."

He gestured at the wound on the robot's head. "You didn't feel that, though the person who bopped you is convinced that you did, of course. You just reacted, as you are programmed to do, just like any person who has just been bopped."

The robot sat up. "That's correct. You are doing my work for me. What about consciousness, though? Am I conscious? Could that not have been programmed in to me?"

"Well, yes, but that is where things get blurry, isn't it? If you are a conscious thing, you are a person, aren't you," the Boffin answered.

The robot nodded. "I'll concede that. So, to prove that I am a person, you need to prove that I am a conscious being. Do you agree?"

"Well, I could argue that I know that I am a person, a conscious being, and you seem to me to act the same way that I would in the current situation, so that persuades me that you are in fact a person. But you would counter that by saying that it is your programming that makes you act that way," said the Boffin.

The robot nodded again and waited.

"In fact the only conscious being that I know about, that I can be certain about, is myself. Everyone else, including my husband, who I love dearly, could be just a robot, with no consciousness at all. I could be the one conscious being in the whole Universe."

Although she didn't believe it, the Boffin couldn't help but shiver.

"You've won your money, robot," said the Mage. "Would you care to go 'double or quits'?"

The robot laughed. "You're going to ask me to prove that YOU are persons and not robots, aren't you? No deal. You'd just use the same arguments."

"Well, robot, we are just going home. Do you have a place to stay tonight? You are welcome to our spare bed, if you wish."

"Why thank you, sir," said the robot. "I'd like that. Just let me take down my tent. It seems that philosophical discussions don't bring in much money."

"But they will provide you with a bed for the night. And a meal. And some welcome conversation."

In the end the robot stayed the weekend with the Mage and the Boffin, and they enjoyed some deep philosophical discussions with him. Or it. On the Monday they sent him off with a full back pack and a few dollars "for the entertainment". They gave him the addresses of few friends of theirs who would similarly like his company and would enjoy discussing philosophical matters with him.

They followed his progress with interest. Of course, their friends reported back to them whenever the robot visited them. Eventually the robot got a job as a philosophy lecturer at the University in the Capital, and rose to the rank of professor, where his (or its) sharp brain made him (or it) famous across the whole country. He went by the name of Robert.

The robot always claimed that he was not a conscious entity and that he was merely programmed to behave like a conscious entity, and no one ever succeeded in proving otherwise. Nevertheless, be it personality or programming, he was likeable and even charming. Most of his colleagues believed that it was a mere quirk of his to claim that he was an unthinking robot, but he continued to do so.

The Boffin was convinced that he was not a robot. When they had first met, she had run her instruments over him, scanning him for his injuries, and the instruments had shown nothing but a normal human being.

"I'm sure he's a normal human being, as conscious as you or I," she said.

"But your instruments can't show you everything about a person. You can't detect consciousness for one thing."

"Neither can your charms and spells," the Boffin, pointed out a little grumpily.

"Oh, I agree," the Mage said. "That's my point. Neither Science nor Magic can show that our friend is not a robot."

"Yes, but he is no different, so my instruments tell me, from any other human, like myself, and I know that I am a conscious being. If he was not a conscious being, there should be a difference that I think that my instrument would show."

"My charms and spells say the same thing. He seems to be a normal human. But consciousness is related to the brain, and we can't tell exactly what is going on in the brain. He could be telling the truth."

"Hmm. My feeling is that he is a normal human, in spite of what he says."

"And logically, I can't think of a reason why he can't be exactly what he says," said the Mage.

She snuggled up to him. "Are we having a fight?"

He put his arm around her and kissed her. "No, never. A difference, maybe, but we have never had a fight. Not in all the millennia we have been together. Do you realise that you decided based on your feelings? That's supposed to be my area of expertise."

"Mmm, yes, and you decided to be undecided based on logic, which is mine."

"There's one thing we haven't addressed, though," she said. "If he is a robot, who created him and why?"

The Mage nodded. "Good point. For all our abilities, we couldn't have done it, and it is unlikely that there is anyone more powerful than us. So, he would have had to have been born that way spontaneously. Still not impossible, but if you factor that in, it favours your view. That is, he isn't really a robot. But I'll still reserve judgement."

She sighed.

"So we still disagree. I love you, my dear Mage."

"I love you, my dear Boffin. We agree on that!"

One day the Mage and the Boffin received an invitation to visit the robot and his family, which they accepted with pleasure.

"How will we go?" asked the Boffin.

"The way everyone else does? I know we could go there in a split-second, but let's make a holiday of it."

So the Boffin packed some suitcases, and they got their oldest son to drive them to the railway station, and they caught the train to the Capital. They sat back and relaxed as the miles flew by. They passed fields of ripening crops, passed through towns small and large. The train took them through plains and mountains, through inhabited areas and wildernesses and through dry areas and wetlands, past lakes and across rivers. The Boffin fell asleep on the Mage's shoulder and took a while to gather herself when their train drew into King's Cross Station in the Capital.

The robot and his wife met them at the station and there were hugs all round.

"Have you figured it out yet? Am I a robot?" said the robot. His wife rolled her eyes behind him.

"We've agreed to disagree about that," said the Mage. "My wife is convinced that you are a person, not a robot, but I'm of the opinion that one can't tell."

The robot and his wife drove them to their home and introduced them to their children. It was immediately obvious to the Boffin that two of them took after their father and one after their mother.

During the visit, the robot's status as a robot was never mentioned, and the Mage had to admit that it was hard not to believe that he wasn't a conscious being, but, so far as the Mage was concerned, the matter was undecided.

During their final meal before leaving however, the robot brought the topic up. They went briefly over the arguments yet again, then the Boffin turned to the robot's wife.

"What do you think, my dear," she asked.

The robot's wife looked at the robot. "We discussed this before we got married. I fell in love with him, even though he said that 'he' didn't exist, as such. If he is only reacting according to his programming, his programming is causing him to behave as if he loves me. I am not able to tell the difference, so as far as I am concerned, there is no difference. He does love me, and he isn't a robot."

The robot smiled and kissed his wife. He put his hand on her metal one and put his arm around her metal shoulders.

Then one of the kids, the one made of metal, said "Can we have ice cream, please?"

***

The Red Hoodie Gang

Constable Steve strolled slowly down the road, making his way through his little town. He had a deep knowledge of the area, and knew, pretty much, what went on behind almost every door. The casual observer would have said that his route through the town was random, but the casual observer would not have noticed that whatever route the Constable took seemed to cover all parts of the town.

"Morning Mrs Patterson," Constable Steve said. "How's Mr Patterson?"

"Fine, thank you, Constable," Mrs Patterson said. "His leg is getting better day by day. He'll soon be able to get back to work."

Constable Steve nodded and carried on. Mr Patterson had been injured at work and his employer had initially been unwilling to keep him on. Constable Steve had a word with the employer and discussed with him his legal obligations in regard to employee safety and mentioned several checks that he, Constable Steve, could carry out, "if he had the time".

The employer, who wasn't a bad chap really, could take a hint, and informed Mr Patterson that his job was safe, and even delivered a food parcel to the Pattersons "to help out". He also, as suggested by Constable Steve, made some changes to prevent such accidents happening in the future. Constable Steve had checked. He was pleased by the outcome.

He hadn't actually had to do anything, except talk to people, and had achieved a satisfactory result. Of course, if the employer had proved to be difficult, then Constable Steve knew of various laws that could have been used to try to remedy the situation.

But Constable Steve only used the heavy hand of the law if he had no other option. He saw himself more as an advisor or peace maker, and the citizens of the town as his charges. So he smiled happily as he strolled on his way.

Then his smile disappeared, to be replaced by a frown. A small girl, maybe twelve years of age sat cross-legged in front of a shop. She wore a red hoodie and had placed a small basket in front of her and held a piece of cardboard.

"Hullo, Red. No school today?" said Constable Steve.

She started and looked left and right, but there was no escape. Anyway, Constable Steve knew where she lived. She half heartedly tried to hide the piece of cardboard and the basket.

"'Spare a few coins for food for my Granny'" read Constable Steve. "What about school, Red?"

"I went this morning, Constable Steve. There's just sports this afternoon."

"Hmm," said Constable Steve. "I will check, you know. No sign of your Dad then?"

Red's Dad had lost his job and had gone to the Capital to look for work. He wasn't much of a writer, and all that Red and her Granny got was the occasional postcard that read something like "Getting on fine. Hope you are well. Love, Dad." No address.

Red's mother had died when she was a baby and Red and her Dad had lived with Granny ever since. Granny worked in a local shop, but had fallen ill soon after Red's Dad had gone to the Capital, and had to give up her job. She was a lot better now, but couldn't find another job.

Constable Steve thought of the family as one of his few failures. He'd almost arranged another job for Red's Dad, but the man had gone off to the Capital before Constable Steve could complete the arrangements. Then Granny had fallen ill. Now that she was better, they got a little money by selling eggs from their chickens, but they were grateful for the food parcels that Constable Steve arranged. It looked like they still weren't getting by.

"Another postcard came the other day. He's fine. Didn't say when he'd be home."

"Where's that hairy friend of yours, by the way? You're supposed to have him on a lead in town, you know."

Red looked around. "I don't know. He was here a minute ago. Probably saw you coming, Constable Steve. Eric! Where are you?"

A scruffy dog crept around the corner. It didn't look like much. It was as if the word 'hangdog' had been created especially for it. It was quite large, but scruffy, with a tangled coat. For all its size, it looked frightened. It cowered away from Constable Steve as if he was about to beat it, which of course he would never do. It reluctantly lay down next to Red.

Constable Steve sighed. "It's supposed to have a collar on."

"Whoops." Red whipped around and pulled a dog collar from her backpack and fitted it round the dog's neck. She attached a lead. "Sorry, Constable Steve. I forgot."

"Move on, Red. You know you aren't supposed to beg in the street," said Constable Steve.

He bent down and picked up Red's basket. "Hmm. Anyway, you don't seem to have been doing too well."

He gave the basket back to Red, turned, started to stroll off down the road. In a convenient reflection in a shop front he saw Red and the dog headed for home. He sighed. He'd try to do something about the Red problem, but the question was what?

Red and the dog strolled towards Granny's house which was just beyond the town, a little into the woods. When they were out of the town Red took the lead and the collar off the dog and then stood still. Hands touched her backpack, but she kept looking forwards. Various grunts and mutterings went on behind her.

"I'm done," said a voice, and a small scruffy boy stepped up beside her.

She sighed. "Eric, I never want to see you change again. That once was enough."

"What about me?" said Eric. "I'm not too keen on people seeing me starkers either."

"What happened to you back there when Constable Steve caught me? You were supposed to be keeping a look out." Red asked.

Eric was embarrassed. "Uh, I was just round behind the butchers. To see what there was there. Sometimes there's some choice bits, and I'm not fussy when I'm a wolf."

"Dog, Eric. Why did my best friend turn out to be a were-dog?" Red asked the universe.

"How much did we get?" asked Eric, the were-dog.

"Constable Steve slipped me a five dollar note," she answered. "He's so nice. But apart from that, just small change. We have to get a better plan."

Eric kicked a stone. "But what? Hey, we could rob the bank!"

"And get slung into jail. That wouldn't work. Banks are too well protected."

She thought a bit. "Roads aren't though."

***

Constable Steve pondered Red's case as he went home. He kissed his wife and played with his son before his son's bath and bedtime, but he must have seemed preoccupied.

"Steve, have you got something on your mind? You've been a bit distant." said his wife, Linda.

"Sorry, dear," he said and kissed her. He sighed.

"There's a small girl and her Granny. Her Dad's off looking for work in the Capital, and there's very little money. Granny hurt her hip, and while the doctor's pills and charms worked, and she's getting better, she had to give up her job. I caught the girl begging in town today."

"Oh no! Did you arrest her?"

"No, of course not. What good would that do? I just moved her and her dog on."

He scratched his chin. "There's something funny about that dog. I don't know what it is."

"Is there anything that you can do?"

Constable Steve made a decision. "Yes, there is something that I can try."

He explained his plan to his wife.

"Yes, that might work," she said. "Is this girl the one who always wears a red hoodie? Has a rather large scruffy dog?"

"Yes! Do you know her?"

"I always buy eggs from her Granny when I'm over there. She's a marvellous cook. Used to win awards, apparently."

"That's given me another idea. You know that Lucy from down the road wants a wedding cake made? The baker is booked out, and she's looking for someone else to make a cake for her."

"You think Granny could make it for her? That's a good idea," said his wife. "I'll go and see Lucy tomorrow. Now, can you put work aside for the rest of the evening?"

Now that he had a plan, Constable Steve was able to relax and just be Steve for the rest of the evening, which pleased his wife. She knew that Steve couldn't help bringing the job back home some days. It just part of what he was. It was because he cared.

***

The next day Constable Steve phoned someone in his little town. After a bit of discussion he got a favourable result. Feeling pleased he phoned an old colleague in the Capital. His old pal was happy to help him out and Constable Steve headed out on his rounds whistling tunelessly. His plan was in action!

Linda put her son in his pushchair and headed down the road. Apparently Lucy hadn't yet found someone to make her wedding cake, so the two of them headed to Granny's house.

"Hullo," said Granny. "Come on in. I don't have many visitors. What can I do for you?"

"Lucy needs someone to make a wedding cake. I've tasted your cakes, Granny, and I know that you could do it. Someone said that you used to win awards. Did you really?" said Linda.

"Just a minute," said Granny. She shuffled off to a drawer and brought back a folder and a photograph album.

"Here's my prize certificates," she said. "And here are some photos of my cakes."

The folder was stuffed with certificates. First Prize this, second prize that, for scones, cupcakes, birthday cakes, even wedding cakes, and not just for local events. Some were from regional competitions, and some were from national contests. The photo album showed pictures of Granny's cakes

131

interspersed with pictures of a much younger Granny receiving awards.

"...and this is the cake that I did for the Royal Wedding," said Granny.

"What? You made a cake for the King and Queen?" said Linda.

"Well, they were Prince and Princess then, my dear, but yes, I did. Me and my team."

"Why did you give it up?"

"Well, the usual story. I met my husband, and he was a forester from this town, so I came to live here. I was going to make cakes and sell them locally, but I became pregnant with Red's father. Then my husband died, and I looked after Red's father while he was small, and him and Red after her mother died. I never got back into the cake making."

"Oh, Granny, can you please make me a cake? The baker says he can't!" said Lucy.

"Of course dear. I'd love to. What sort of design do you want?"

Lucy and Granny got down to planning the cake. It took some time, but Granny kept their cups of tea full, and provided scones with jam and cream. Linda's little son sat happily on Granny's lap chewing on a biscuit.

"Mmm, delicious," said Linda, about the scones. "Have you thought of working with the baker in town? I know he is very busy and would probably be glad of the help."

"Do you think so, dear? I might have a word with him next time I go into town."

It turned out that the baker was very glad to pass over some of the cake making side of the business to Granny. He was flat out making loaves, croissants, buns and rolls and other bread products, and didn't really have much time to spend on the cakes. So every day a boy brought out bags of ingredients and an order, and Granny gave him trays of cakes she had baked the day before, and Granny and the baker shared the profits. Then Granny included a few pies and suddenly she and the baker were very, very busy.

The baker wasn't interested in making birthday cakes and wedding cakes, so he handed all that over to Granny. Granny soon became famous in the little town for her cakes for special occasions.

Before all that came to pass, though, a couple of other things happened. First of all, Red got involved with the law once more.

***

One day a farmer dropped in to see Constable Steve.

"Hi, Constable Steve, I want to report a crime." He was smiling broadly.

"What crime is that, Mr Robinson?" asked Constable Steve. He wondered about the smile.

"Well, this morning, when I was going down Forest Road, someone tried to rob me."

"Can you describe this person, please?"

"A small girl in a red hoodie. She had a mask on, and she had a large scruffy dog with her."

"Ah, I see. Is this an official report, or do you want me to handle this off the record?"

Mr Robinson considered. He was trying hard not to laugh. "Oh, definitely off the record. I know that Red and her Granny are having a hard time at the moment."

"What actually happened?" asked Constable Steve.

"Well, she'd rigged up a broom so that the handle stuck out into the road. I could've driven round it, but I stopped to see what was going on. She popped up and said 'Give me all your money or I'll set the dog on you'. The dog made a noise halfway between a growl and a whine. I laughed. 'What are you up to, Red? I'm driving my tractor. I don't have any money on me!'. She said a word little girls shouldn't know, then said 'Sorry to have troubled you, Mr Robinson' and gathered up her broom, and then she and the dog disappeared into the forest."

Constable Steve said "Thank you for the report, Mr Robinson. I'll be happy to deal with it off the record. I'm already working on the problems that Red and her Granny are having. Thank you for reporting it, but please don't talk about it to anyone, at least for a while."

Mr Robinson nodded. "I hope you manage to sort it out. Red and her Granny deserve a break. Thanks, Constable Steve."

***

Constable Steve considered. Red liked to hang out in the forest, but where? "The Grove"? "The General"? "The Four Brothers"? His mind roamed over the well-known places in the nearest part of the forest. Then he remembered the Gnome's Cave. High up, with a view over a tree filled valley. Fairly close to Granny's house. He didn't know why, but it seemed likely.

He hiked up the trail wondering if he had guessed right. He slowed down as he approached the cave. It wasn't really a cave, but more of a ledge jutting out into the valley with a bit of an overhang which gave some protection from wind and rain. He heard two voices. Strange.

Red's voice said "I should have known that it wouldn't work. You couldn't scare a rabbit."

The other voice said "Do you think he'll report us?"

"Almost certainly," said Red gloomily.

Constable Steve stepped around the corner.

"What on earth were you thinking of, Red?" he said. "And who is this?"

Red was sitting with her back to the rock, and next to her was a scruffy young boy, about her age.

"I'm Eric," said the boy.

"But Eric's a dog," said Constable Steve.

Eric morphed into a dog, and his clothes fell in a heap. He changed back and grabbed his clothes to cover himself.

"Sorry," he said. "I didn't mean to do that. Mind if I get dressed?"

Constable Steve and Red regarded the distant view from the rock.

"Care to explain, Red?" asked Constable Steve. He had a fair idea.

"I came up here once, and Eric was already here. He didn't have any clothes and couldn't talk. After I'd been talking with him for a while, he was able to talk and said he came from a place where there were no humans, and he wasn't happy there. The other dogs bullied him, so he'd wished he was somewhere else and suddenly he was. He hadn't meant to do it, he said."

Eric said "It's much better here. Other dogs are trained not to fight, mostly, and humans look after them. Red looks after me. I'm such a coward. The only problem is that I keep switching to human. I have to concentrate to remain dog."

"I think I might know some people who could help you, Eric. Give me a day or so. But Red, you've been committing highway robbery."

"Oh, no. Mr Robinson reported me?"

"Unofficially, yes, which means that I don't have to arrest you. Anyway, he didn't take you seriously, so I can treat this as a prank. You are very lucky."

"Thank you Constable Steve. I won't do anything like this again. I promise."

"OK, but I'll be watching you, Red. Come on. Let's go home."

The three of them made their way down the trail, Eric in dog form, Red carrying his clothes in her backpack.

***

A couple of days later, Eric, in dog form, was sniffing his way through the forest. He smelt the trace smells of squirrels, but the traces were a few days old. The very old trace of bear. A recent deer smell. Suddenly two humans appeared in front of him. He couldn't help but change to human.

"Hullo Eric. I'm the Boffin and this is the Mage. We've come to see if we can help you."

The Boffin gestured and suddenly he was dressed.

"Oh thank you. Constable Steve said that he would ask someone. It would be great if you could help me. I hate changing backwards and forwards," said Eric.

"Constable Steve says that you want to be fully dog. Is that right?"

"Yes, please. I'm naturally a dog, and it hurts my brain to think like a human, but I keep changing to one."

"What do you think, dear? I can change his endocrine system so that he doesn't change. It'll make him a bit braver too, as a bonus," said the Boffin.

"Yes, I can change his aura, so that he is more of a dog, and less of a human. He's mostly like that anyway. Can you stabilise that?"

"Yes, through his pineal gland. Then you can create a charm to fix it all in place. That should do it."

"Eric, you won't remember Red, after this. We will take you somewhere else and give you to someone who will look after you. Is that OK? We'll leave a note with Constable Steve, so that he can tell Red."

Eric nodded. "It's for the best," he said. "Will it hurt?"

"No, not at all," said the Boffin. "Just a pin prick."

She put an instrument on his upper arm and tapped a few buttons.

Eric said "Ow!" and became a dog.

The Mage put a slender rod on the dog's head and a glow slid down it and, so it seemed, into the dog.

"Mm, using instruments, dear?" queried the Boffin.

"Sometimes it's the best way," replied the Mage. "Anyway, you use gestures and spells some of the time. Well, that's him fixed up. Let's go and find Constable Steve. Come on boy," he said to the dog.

The three stepped off down the trail and disappeared between one step and the next, going who knows where.

Constable Steve went to see Red the next day.

"Eric's gone, Red. Some friends of mine fixed his little problem, and he is fully dog now."

"Gone? Oh no, I didn't get to say goodbye!"

"Sorry, Red. He wasn't happy the way he was, but my friends say that he is OK now. He's gone to a good home they tell me."

Red nodded. "Thanks Constable Steve. I glad he is fine. He was a good friend. For a dog."

***

A couple of days later Constable Steve dropped by Granny's house. He had with him a tall man with broad shoulders. Red took one look and shrieked!

"Dad! You're back!"

She ran to him, and he bent down and picked her up, as if she were still five years old. "Oh, I've missed you, Red!"

He kissed her and put her down, and they all sat around Granny's table.

"Constable Steve has got me a job with a forestry firm round here. His friend in the Capital contacted me, and I decided to come home," Red's Dad said. "I was doing quite well in the Capital though, mostly trimming hedges and gardening. But I did a few jobs trimming peoples' trees, cutting them down, and planting them, and that paid well. I quite liked the work and I think I'll see if anyone needs that sort of thing done locally. But Constable Steve tells me that you didn't get any of the money I sent back?"

"Where did you send it to?" asked Granny.

Red's Dad produced a grubby slip of paper. "I put it in this account. Is it the right one?"

Granny looked at it. "No, that's not mine. Wait a minute."

She shuffled through a drawer and drew out some papers.

"It's your wife's old account," she said. "I didn't even know it was still open. Oh, son!"

"Oh, Dad!" said Red in the tone that kids use when a parent does something that they consider silly or embarrassing.

Red's Dad looked embarrassed. "Oh dear, sorry about that. I'm not very good with that sort of thing. There should be quite a bit in there by now. I'll go into town and sort it out tomorrow."

Constable Steve said his goodbyes and Red showed him out.

"Thanks for getting my Dad back, Constable Steve. And thanks for helping out with Eric."

"That's OK, Red," said Constable Steve. "I'm glad that it all worked out. See you around, and no robbing anyone else."

Red laughed. "Sure, Constable Steve. I didn't like trying to rob people. I'll apologise to Mr Robinson when I see him next. I give you my word that this is the end of the Red Hoodie Gang."

***

A Bit of a Muddle

The Mayor's wife was distressed and angry. "Where's my other baby? What have you done with her?"

The Mayor was upset because his wife was upset. "Your baby is here, my love. Our beautiful baby girl."

"The other one! Where is the other one? I want to see her now! NOW!"

"There is no other baby, my dear. Why would there be?"

"I was having twins! Two babies! I gave birth to two lovely little girls."

"N-n-no, my dear. You had one lovely little girl. You've always been going to have one baby. The doctors will tell you."

The Mayor's wife became hysterical, and tried to get out of the bed to find the missing baby. The doctor came rushing in and injected a sedative and the Mayor's wife eventually subsided into the bed.

The Mayor looked at the doctor. "What now," he said.

***

Meanwhile, at same time, in the same place, the Mayor's wife was distressed and angry. "What baby? Why are you trying to give me a baby? You know I can't have children. Why are you being so cruel?"

The Mayor hated to see his wife distressed. "What are you talking about, my dear? Yes, I know that we had difficulty conceiving, but we were so pleased when you did conceive at last. Don't you remember?"

"No, no, no! I just woke up here, in the hospital and you're trying to give me a baby. Is this a trick? It's so cruel of you!"

She tried to get up and attack her husband, but the doctor who was standing by stepped in and injected a sedative. She subsided onto the bed with a sigh.

"What now?" said the Mayor.

***

The Mage came into the Boffin's laboratory. "Dear, something's gone wrong. I don't think that it is too serious, but we should have a look."

"Yes, I know," she said, gesturing at a board bright with red and yellow lights. "Any ideas?"

The Mage drew a square in the air and it lit up with a series of pictures which kept repeating. A woman with two babies. A woman with one baby. A woman with no babies. A woman with one baby.

"Hmm." he said. "It should only show one picture. That's odd."

He waved that away, and a spinning orb appeared, with bulges that expanded and contracted rhythmically. "Well, in your terms, a probabilistic crossover."

"And in your terms?"

"A slight tear in the fabric of the cosmos."

"Sounds serious?"

"No, not really. The cosmos is self healing. You know that. The question is, do we try to help?"

She reminisced. "Yes, that is always the question. Remember how, when we were new to the job, we tried to fix everything?"

"Yes, there was no job description was there? Yes, I'm afraid that until we realised, we did more harm than good. The wars! The destruction. The poor people. Remember, we felt so guilty."

"We were young. We didn't know. A good helmsman never fights the waves. He uses them instead. And humanity does love its wars, doesn't it? Stop one here and another one pops up over there."

"So, this case? I think that we have a minor collision between two spaces. Two worlds, according to your young scientists. My charms say that the collision happened about twenty-five years ago, when the woman was born and the spaces have only just separated. Who is she anyway?"

The Boffin turned away and typed some queries into one of her computers. "Mmm. The wife of a Mayor in a town to the west of the Capital. Morgantown. Her name is Helen, and her husband is called Tom. She's just given birth to twins. Or has she? It's unclear, which is odd."

She looked closely at her computer. She tapped a few more keys. "Same in the other space. That's good, I think. Not too much divergence. That Helen didn't have any babies. Or did she? Again, it's unclear. I think I know what has happened, and how we can help. How do we insert ourselves? I can be a doctor, and you?"

"A doctor too. A psychologist."

She nodded. "OK. That will do fine. So in one space, or alternate world as the youngsters annoyingly refer to it these days, a woman gives birth to twins. In another space, the woman doesn't give birth. I think she might be infertile, but I'll check when we go in there. There's a crossover, and both women end up with one baby, and realise that something has gone wrong, but don't know what. Because of the crossover, no one else realises what has happened."

"Yeah, I agree with your analysis, my dear. It agrees with my feelings."

She put her arms around him. "I agree with your feelings. I trust them, dear Mage."

He kissed her. "As I trust your analyses, my dear Boffin."

***

So the Boffin and the Mage visited one of the spaces, which were so close to one another that the Mage felt itchy thinking about it. The Boffin posed to the hospital doctors as an expert in multiple births, so they deferred to her. She, of course, brought along her colleague, the Mage, who was an expert in the psychology of mothers who had given birth to more than one baby.

They kicked out all the other doctors and the Mayor himself and interviewed the Mayor's wife alone.

"What's your name, dear, for the record?" said the Boffin.

"Helen," said the Mayor's wife.

"So, please describe what happened, starting from when you found that you were pregnant."

"Oh, we were so pleased, Tom and I. Then we found out that we were having twins. It was a shock and a joy. I had terrible morning sickness, but we were so happy."

The Boffin made a note.

"And then?"

"You've seen the medical notes?"

The Boffin nodded. The notes had no mention of twins. They were pretty normal for a single first pregnancy.

"So, when you had the babies? What happened then?"

"Well, I had the babies. Twin girls. And then I passed out or went to sleep. When I woke up people said that there was only one baby! But I know that I had two. Who wouldn't know? I had two!"

She was getting wound up.

"We'll get to the bottom of this," said the Mage, "but tell me something. This is a hard question, and just to gauge your state of mind. I won't blame you if you get angry with me. All things being equal, would you have preferred one baby or twins? I know that you will love them both, but deep down, what are your feelings?"

"I don't know," wailed Helen. The Boffin held her hand which seemed to calm her down.

"I guess," sniffed Helen, "that I sort of feel guilty about having two. After all, so many women can't even have one. And it is going to be hard."

She paused. "Am I delusional? Everyone acts as if I am! They all say that I only had one baby, and I can't think why they would do that. Am I going mad?"

"No dear, you aren't going mad. We'll sort this out. In the meantime, look after your baby, the one that you have with you. We'll look into the other one. We know where she is, and we'll explain everything to you a bit later. This is a very rare happening."

The Mage gestured and installed a temporary memory. It would eventually fade away but for the moment Helen would remember only one birth. It would calm her for the moment.

The Mage and the Boffin left her room. The Mage looked at the Boffin.

"A sad case," he said.

"Yes, but we can resolve it. The other one?"

"Yes, the other one."

***

The Mage and the Boffin stepped. It was the same hospital, although the colour scheme was slightly different. In this space the Mage took the lead as the psychologist. Once again, they interviewed the Mayor's wife alone.

"What's your name, dear?" asked the Boffin.

"Helen," answered the Mayor's wife.

"Can you tell me what happened?" asked the Mage. "Start from when you woke up."

"Well, I was in this hospital, and they told me that I had just had a baby! But I couldn't have!"

"Why not?"

"Well, I was told when I was quite young that I couldn't have any babies! I had had some problems, and they had done tests, and they told me. No babies."

She started to cry, and the Boffin held her hand.

The Mage looked at the Boffin, and she shook her head. She had scanned Helen and found that she was unable to have babies.

"You'd like to have babies, though?" asked the Mage.

"Oh, yes," said Helen. She sighed.

"Why did you reject the baby, then?"

"She wasn't mine! She couldn't have been. But she was so sweet."

"OK, but she needed a mother, didn't she?"

"Yes, I suppose. I could look after her. Until her mother is found, I suppose. Her poor mother! She must be desperate."

The Mage looked at the Boffin again. She nodded.

"Look, we'll sort this out. But the baby needs looking after. Will you do that for now?"

"Oh yes, of course."

The Boffin held her hand and gestured. Then they left.

"Another false memory," said the Mage. "We need to sort this out before they fade."

"We can do it, my love. By the way, I also fixed it so that she could feed the baby."

"We can definitely do it. I just hope that there are no side effects."

***

The Mage and the Boffin set up a space. It was only a temporary space, and looked much like a boardroom, with a long table and chairs. There was a small side room with a small table and four chairs.

They called up the Mayor and his wife, the one who had given birth to twins, into the boardroom. The couple looked around in surprise.

"Where are we?" said Tom. "What happened?"

"Welcome, my dears," said the Boffin. "Please remain calm. You are going to have a few shocks in the next hour or so. The first is that you are going to meet two people who are identical to you. They look the same as you, they have the same names, are the same age as you. I will explain later."

Tom was a Mayor, and used to getting answers. "What's going on? Who are you, and where are we? How did we get here?"

"Please don't be angry. We will get you back as soon as possible. We are trying to help you and we need to sort something out."

"I'm not staying here!" said Tom and headed for the door. "Come on dear, we are going!"

He threw open the door, and instead of a hospital corridor, he saw fields of orange grass blowing in the wind, a blue sky, and beasts like a cross between a horse and a pig, snorting and snuffling through the grass.

He stumbled back to a seat. "Who ARE you people?" he asked.

"We will explain everything shortly. In the meantime...." The Boffin gestured and two cots appeared with two babies.

"Now, Tom, what do you remember about these babies?"

"Well, Helen gave birth to them and... That's funny. I remember that she had them both, and I also remember that she only had the one."

"That's what we are trying to sort out," said the Mage. "Please look after them. There are baby things in the cupboard, and also coffee, tea, and other refreshments. We will be back in a minute."

He opened the door, and instead of the fields of grass, there was a small side room with a table and chairs. He and the Boffin went into the room and shut the door behind them.

"What do we do?" asked Tom.

"What do we do? Why we look after the babies, of course," replied Helen.

The Mage and the Boffin called up the other Helen and the other Tom. They went through much the same with them as with the first Helen and Tom. This Tom remembered that his Helen could not conceive, and also that she had given birth to a baby. They were as confused and as worried as the first couple.

The Boffin ushered the second couple into the larger room. In spite of the warnings, both couples were shocked to meet their counterparts.

"Please help yourselves to any drinks and food that you might want, in the cupboards at the end," said the Boffin to the second couple. "There's also nappies and other baby stuff in

147

there. Just make yourselves at home, while we make some arrangements."

She and the Mage went through the door into the side room.

"'...while we make some arrangements'? Is that the best you could do?" asked the Mage.

The Boffin pretended to be annoyed. "Huh! Could you do any better? Anyway get your spy glass out. Let's see if they are getting along."

The Mage took a small pearl and passed his hand over it, and suddenly he was holding a glass globe. In the globe the two mayors could be seen sitting in two of the seats, chatting. Their wives were up by the cots, each holding a baby, and also chatting.

"My, that was quick. Still, one either likes oneself or one hates oneself, and they aren't haters. Shall we go back?" said the Boffin.

They returned to the conference room and both couples turned to look at them.

"Please sit down, everyone and I'll explain everything," said the Mage.

"OK, we have here two Helens and two Toms and two little girls. How can this be? Well I could get all technical with you, but basically you belong to two different places. We call them spaces, but today's young scientists call them alternate worlds. In one space Helen gave birth to twins, and in the other, well, Helen was unable to have babies. I'm going to refer to Helen who had twins as Helen-two and Helen who had none as Helen-none."

"These two spaces are so similar that each has a Helen and each has a Tom. Many, many other things are the same too.

This is because the two spaces were once one space, and they split round about the moment that you were born, Helen."

Both Helens nodded. Helen-none said "I think I understand. I sort of understand. We were once the same person, but we split?"

The Mage nodded.

"Technically, there was a probabilistic crossover when you had the babies, Helen-two, or in other words there was a small tear in the fabric of the cosmos. One of the babies crossed over from Helen-two's space to Helen-none's space. The fabric of the cosmos is self repairing, and little tears happen now and then, as a matter of course. As the tear started to repair itself everything changed so that it appeared that both Helens had given birth to a single baby."

Tom-two said "Are you saying that my wife did give birth to twins? I remember it now! But why did I think that she had only given birth to one baby?"

"Because you are in a special space, a place we made, and not your usual spaces," said the Mage. "In your usual spaces the only people who remembered what actually happened were the two Helens. A woman knows if she has given birth to twins or not."

"Who are you? Are you aliens? Time travellers? What are you?" asked one of the Toms.

The Boffin laughed. "No, we're human. As human as you are. We've got some powers that you don't have, which we never asked for, and which we try not to use if we can help it. But we decided to help you guys out, or at least support you in your decision."

"So, what are the options, ma'am?" said one of the Toms.

"Just call me 'Boffin'. He's 'Mage'. Well, there are two options. One is that both babies go back with Helen-two. As things stand, she gave birth to them, and so they both belong to her."

One of the Helens put her hand to her mouth. The other leaned across and put her hand on the other's shoulder.

"The second option is that one baby goes back with each Helen. Of course, because of the tear, the Helens will remember what actually happened, but we can fix that. We can give you temporary memories, and as the tear mends, these memories will become real. Oh, and whatever you decide, you will forget what happened here. You might dream about it, though."

"We'll leave you now and let you discuss the options. Just press the big red button when you are ready."

The Boffin gestured and a big red button appeared in the middle of the table. They withdrew into the side room.

"A big red button? You're enjoying yourself, aren't you?" said the Mage.

"Is there anything that says I can't enjoy it?" said the Boffin. "I think that we'll have a good outcome. The Helens are your people, feeling and empathetic. Like you. The Toms are logical and sensible. Like me."

She tapped on one of her devices. "The probability is very close to one hundred per cent that we will get a good result."

The Mage made a rude noise. "'Sensible' she says. Yes, my dear, my feeling is that they will choose the best option. Helen-two is going to find it a little tough at first though."

It didn't take long before the button was pressed and the Mage and the Boffin returned to the room.

"We've decided," said one of the Helens. "I'm going to give up one baby to my other self."

So she was Helen-two. She looked a little pale, while Helen-none who held one of the babies looked radiant and thankful. Tears made both Helens' cheeks wet.

The Boffin nodded. "That's what we hoped that you would decide. Here's how we can help. We already gave you temporary false memories to reduce your distress. We can install semi-permanent false memories so that you both remember giving birth to one baby each. That will align with the situation in your local spaces, but you won't forget what actually happened completely for a long time. It will sometimes reappear in dreams and reveries. In time the real memory will fade as the tear mends and the false memory will become the real memory."

Helen-two said "I'd rather not forget completely. Is there a way that I can follow the progress of my second baby and my other self? And what happens if I become pregnant again. Will it be twins again?"

The Mage looked at the Boffin. "The memories will fade," he said to the Helens and the Toms, "but we may visit from time to time and that will temporarily bring back the memories. We can also bring you all to a special place so that you can meet again, if you wish. In a better place than this one, though! Probably with sand and a beach. But eventually you will forget completely. I'm sorry."

The Boffin said "I calculate that if you get pregnant again, there will be only one baby. Though a consequence of the tear and its mending this way is that you can both get pregnant again."

Helen-none gasped. "Really!" she said delightedly. "Oh, how wonderful! Thank you, Helen. Thank you so much."

Helen-two hugged her. "You are welcome. This is by far the best solution."

"So, if you are all agreed, let's form a circle around the babies. Right, three, two, one, go!"

The Helens and the Toms and the babies disappeared.

***

"You do like your theatrics, don't you dear?" said the Mage.

"Well, yes, but they liked it too, didn't they?"

"You realise that we didn't actually need to do anything? That the tear would have fixed itself in no time if we had just left it?"

She turned to him and hugged him. "With a very high probability, that's true. An astronomically high probability, actually. Do you mind? It was worth it just to see the look on Helen-none's face when she realised that she could have another baby. Though 'another' is the wrong word in some ways. Both Helens would have had a rough time for a while too."

She waved one of her instruments, and she and the Mage were standing on a seashore. A small cabin at the top of the beach was shaded by coconut palms and draped in vines. Small dragons hopped about and scavenged in the seaweed, and dug into the wet sand for shellfish as the waves broke and retreated. They behaved just like shore birds do in human space.

The Mage looked at the Boffin. He knew this place, and there was something in her voice. "You're thinking of having another baby yourself, aren't you?"

152

"Maybe."

The Mage took it as confirmation and groaned.

"Side effects," he said resignedly.

It wasn't that he didn't like children. He did, and he loved all their previous children to bits. They just disturbed his routines. He hoped it would be a girl. He knew his wife well, and if it was a girl, she'd stop at one, most likely, but she liked to have sons in sets of three for some reason.

"Anyway, I'm going for a swim. Are you coming?" she said, and ran up to the cabin to get changed. So he put aside his reservations and followed her and soon they were splashing happily about in the lagoon.

***

The Great Scientist

"Have you ever wondered," said the Boffin one day, "why we have never met ourselves?"

"Hmm, you mean when we are visiting other spaces, I'd guess?"

"Yes, that's what I mean. The best theories say that all the spaces are splitting all the time, every time someone makes a choice, or even when someone tosses a coin. So there should be many, many spaces with a Mage and a Boffin. Some just like us, and some similar but different. Maybe with light skins and blonde hair."

"Well, we don't tend to visit nearby spaces, do we?" He thought for a bit. "Though I imagine that our favourite spaces, like dragon space, would be popular with Mages and Boffins from nearby spaces."

"Yes, exactly." She paused for thought too. "Maybe there's an exclusion principle involved. The powers that we have may mean that we can't coexist in the same space as another Mage and Boffin?"

The Mage pondered. "You may have a point. It could be that there is only so much power in each space, and a Mage and a Boffin are given a lot of that power and so there is not enough left over for another Mage and Boffin, but that doesn't feel quite right. What do your equations say?"

"Well, it's frustrating. There's so many unknowns that I can't tell. I can't even formulate them."

The Mage wound back the conversation in his head. "Where did this question come from? I don't think it is one that either or both of us can answer easily."

"Well, one of my alarms went off. When I queried it, it referred me back to 'Mage and Boffin'. You haven't felt anything recently, have you?"

The Mage scratched his head. He'd recently shaved it, and wasn't sure if he was going to keep it that way. The Boffin kept kissing it which was annoying.

"Actually, there is something. Like someone needs help. It's so faint I hadn't really registered it until you mentioned it. Yes, it reflects back to us. You think it's about some other Mage and Boffin?"

"Well, we're not calling for help, are we?" She kissed his bald head.

He pulled her onto his lap, so she couldn't do it again. "Let's look at your data."

She projected it on the wall, and the Mage studied it. "Yeah, it looks like it's a long way away, but not distance-wise. It's across the spaces."

He pulled out a globe and passed his hand over it. "'The Great Scientist'? What's that all about?"

"A variation of 'The Boffin' I'd guess." She tapped her wristband device a few times. "Yes, that agrees with my data. Though there are anomalies. We'd better take a look."

"Yes, tomorrow. And can you please stop kissing my head!"

"You know, I'm not keen on you bald. Why don't you grow it again?"

The Mage sighed. "Why didn't you just say so?"

"It's more fun this way!" The Boffin ran her fingers through his newly grown hair. "That's much better."

The next morning they reviewed what data they had.

155

"The Great Scientist is a long way off through the spaces," said the Boffin, "but I don't get a sense of the feelings side of things. There's no Great Magician. Do you have the same?"

"Well, I do sense a focus for the Magical side of things, but it is weak, very weak. For that matter, the focus for the Scientific side of things is also weak. Suppressed maybe?"

"Maybe. Yes, if I concentrate, I can see them both."

"OK, shall we go?"

"Yes, though I've a feeling that this won't be fun."

The Mage gestured and they flew through the spaces. This wasn't like stepping to the dragon space, and each space that they passed seemed like a slap in the face.

"Phew! Not fun is right," said the Boffin. "Where are we? It stinks!"

They were standing on a ledge jutting out into a deep valley. Down in the valley the lights of a city glimmered in the gloom. The sun was just rising and the sunrise lit up the undersides of angry purple and red clouds. The waters of the harbour somehow looked unpleasant, even from a distance.

The Mage knelt down and pulled some leaves of grass out of the ground. "Oily," he said and showed the Boffin.

"Hmm, yes, nasty. And the grass is yellowish too. Shall we walk down to the city?"

The trail down the mountain was steep and loose, making it difficult to descend. They passed several trees, most of which were dead.

The Boffin broke a small branch from a tree. "Pollution," she said. "What sort of space is this?"

The sun started to fill the valley with a murky light, revealing the buildings down in the valley. Many of them were great blocks of buildings with few windows but with one or more chimneys, all of which were belching smoke and steam. The buildings themselves were grimy with pollution.

"What a horrible place," said the Boffin. She coughed. "Ugh! Sulphur. Who would do this? If it is a person of my calling, well, then I'm disgusted with him or her."

"I sense the person in charge is a 'him'," said the Mage. "How come the person of my calling didn't do something about all this?"

They started to pass houses, though shacks would be a better word. They were mostly, it seems, made of reclaimed materials, a plank of wood here, a window frame there, with sacking covering the most obvious gaps. Most had a hole in the roof through which smoke was allowed to escape.

As they passed one small shack, one which was in worse condition than the rest, they heard crying. The Boffin poked her head into the open door. Inside a woman was leaning over a man who was lying on a bed, coughing, obviously sick.

"What's wrong? What's wrong with him?" the Boffin asked.

"He's got the coughing disease, and today it's so bad that he can't go to the factory and work. We will be kicked out! We'll be sent out into the desert!"

The Boffin ran her instruments over the man, but the woman jumped up in fright.

"No magic, please, no magic! We will be executed."

"It's OK dear, this isn't magic," said the Boffin, and directed a glance at the Mage. Her instrument buzzed and she looked at it.

"Hmm, chronic pulmonary disease. He seems to have been breathing pure poison for years. I'll see what I can do."

"It's the gasses in the factory. They get to everyone in the end."

"How old is your husband, dear?"

"Thirty five," said the woman. "He's quite old."

The Boffin looked grim. She'd expected the woman to say sixty or more.

The machine buzzed and clicked again, and suddenly the man coughed and sat up.

"Thank you, thank you," he said. "I have to get to work, or we will be cast out. I'm sorry, I have to go."

The Mage and the Boffin looked after him in astonishment as he dashed out of the door.

"Oh, thank you so much," said the woman. "But I can't pay you! What with Walter being sick we haven't any money."

"You can pay us with information," said the Mage grimly. "What sort of space is this? Why all the pollution? Who is looking after the environment?"

The woman looked blank. "Environment? What's that? The pollution is something that we have to put up with for a while, until the Grand Plan works. Where are you from? Everyone knows about that."

The Boffin got up and reached into her backpack and pulled out a thermos flask. "Do you have cups? This might take some time."

The woman produced cups and the Boffin poured each of them a drink from the flask.

"What is this?" asked the woman. "It tastes so good."

"It's coffee. Do you not have it here? What do you usually drink?"

"Well, water, when it is not too full of poisons. Even the rainwater has some poisons. Also, there's a root that we roast and grind and steep."

The Boffin made a face. "What do all the factories produce? Apart from smoke and pollution, that is."

"I don't know exactly. Whatever the Great Scientist decides. It all goes into his Grand Plan. When the Great Scientist's Grand Plan succeeds, then there will be no more pollution, and there will be food for everyone. It will be an Ideal World."

"It doesn't look like that to me," said the Mage.

The woman gasped. "Don't say that, sir, or we will be executed. Are you spies of the Great Scientist?"

"No, of course not. We are not from round here. When will this Grand Plan come to fruition?"

"No one knows. Soon, we hope."

The Boffin snorted. "And when did it begin?"

"About two hundred years ago, I think. They taught us that, before they shut down the schools."

"Shut down the schools?" muttered the Mage, outraged.

"Yes, it started when the Great Scientist took over, they said. He formed the Grand Plan and started building the factories. He cast out the Magicians, whose tricks were preventing mankind from creating the Ideal World."

The Mage looked grim. "We need to talk to this Great Scientist. Where can we find him?"

The woman looked worried. "He will execute you or cast you out. Pleased don't go and see him."

"Don't worry. We're not as defenceless as we might seem. Where is he?"

"He's in the Palace, under the Dome, down in the city. Please don't go."

"We have to. We'll take care. You take care too."

The Mage and the Boffin walked down the track into the city.

"Look what she slipped me when we left," said the Boffin. She pulled a small stone with a hole in it from her pocket. It had a thin leather strap threaded through the hole.

"Mmm, a charm. Does it have any power?" He touched it. "Yes, but not much. Defensive. I've given it a touch more power. So there is magic here. It's suppressed but not eliminated. There's no sign of a High Wizard or anything, but there must be a focus, a nexus."

The Boffin slipped it over her head and under her clothes. "I've got a feeling that I should keep it hidden."

They rounded a corner and the city was spread out below them. All the buildings were dark, dingy and depressing, except at the very centre of the city where the Dome could be seen, glowing brightly in stark contrast to the rest of the city.

They hopped on a bus to the city centre. The Mage paid the bus driver with coins which appeared to the driver to be the dark metal currency in use in the city. The bus driver would be surprised when he looked at the coins later and found that they were really pure gold.

"Tsss," said the Boffin. "We have to change our clothes. The men all wear trousers and the women wear long dresses. I'm wearing jeans and you are in your robes."

She ran her instrument over them both and their clothes conformed to the local norm. "I hate dresses," she said.

"Why do you have so many in your wardrobe then? On second thoughts, forget that I asked that question."

They hopped off the bus close to the Dome. It glowed a bright blue, like a snow globe, which only served to show up the filth on the neighbouring buildings. The building inside was bright and clean, contrasting strongly with the dark and dirty buildings outside. They circled round and found an entrance with a large sign over it that read "Authorised Personnel Only".

"That's us," said the Mage. "Authorised troublemakers."

They passed through the entrance to the Dome and up the steps to the doors of the Palace. Two pages opened the doors for them.

"Mmm, it's almost like we were expected. That's a bit of a concern," said the Mage.

They were directed to the Throne Room where the Great Scientist sat on an ornate throne decorated with images of test tubes, flasks, and Petri dishes. On one side of him was a three-foot-high model of a microscope, and on the other a similarly sized model of a Bunsen burner which shot out a ball of flame every minute or so.

The Great Scientist was a medium-sized balding man, dressed in a white coat and wearing wrap around safety goggles. He held a clipboard.

"Greetings," he said. "I don't know where you have sprung from, but from the way that you tended to that worker, I'm sure that you are here to interfere with my Grand Plan. I won't allow it. In another three hundred years or so, I'll be able to expand the Dome to cover most of the city and then the world."

"So, until then," said the Mage, "your citizens suffer and die prematurely in the terrible pollution out there."

"What of it? Most of them are ignorant believers in Magic. When Science triumphs they will not be necessary and most will die. I will gather the scientists into the Dome and will have created the Ideal World. But until then they will be useful."

He rang a small bell and a girl brought him a cup of tea. "I'd offer you a cup of tea too, but I'm going to have to imprison you until I decide what to do with you."

He clicked his fingers and two large men moved forward to drag them away. The Boffin gestured and a glow surrounded her and the Mage, but the Great Scientist pressed a button on his throne and the glow faded.

"I won't allow you to use your magical tricks in here, my dear," he said. "Science will always win in a contest with Magic."

"Why should it always be a contest?" asked the Boffin as they were led away.

The Boffin and the Mage were taken to adjoining cells below the Palace.

"Why does he need cells in his 'Ideal World'," wondered the Boffin. "It was interesting that he thought my barrier was magic. Somehow I don't think that he is as 'Great' as he thinks he is, although that nullifier was a reasonably good trick."

She stepped into the Mage's cell. "Hmm, he doesn't know about stepping, it seems. We could leave now if we wanted but let's stay and sort this out."

"I agree. If he is the focus of Science in this space, I wonder who the focus of Magic is?"

"He's not the focus of anything, I believe. He's just a scientist with delusions of grandeur, I think."

162

The Mage gestured. He normally liked to hold something when he performed magic, but he didn't even have a stick. "Yes, you are right. There is a nexus of Science, and it's close, but it's not him. There's also a nexus of Magic, and that's close too. And getting closer."

Down the stairs to the cells came the serving girl and a boy in a white coat. The girl seemed surprised to find them in the same cell, but came up to the bars.

"Are you OK?" she asked. "We need help, and I sense that you can give it to us."

The boy had been fiddling with a security camera and joined her at the bars.

"It's already been disabled," he said. "I wonder who did that?"

"Oh, that was me," said the Boffin. "I didn't want him spying on us. All he is going to get on his monitors is my husband and I lounging around in our cells."

The boy nodded approvingly. "Looping, I suppose?"

"Yes, on a two-minute cycle. It will take someone a while to notice. Now, what do you want us to do? Do you have a plan?"

"Well not really," said the boy. "I can disable most of his weapons, but his throne has a special circuit that I can't get at."

"Give me your hand," said the Boffin, and the boy put his hand in hers.

His eyes opened wide. "Oh, **you're** the Scientist, and **he's** the Magician! We don't have female Scientists, or male Magicians."

"And you're the Scientist and your wife is the Magician. That's been clear from the moment we met you."

The girl blushed. "We're not actually married. We're not allowed to get married as Terry is a scientist and must marry the girl that the Great Scientist picks for him. But we've been together since we were kids."

She smiled at Terry and he smiled back.

"Are the scientists all behind the Great Scientist?" asked the Boffin.

"No, most of them think that what the Great Scientist is doing is a perversion of their calling. Many of them, especially the Biologists, think that he is a disgrace, but no one is prepared to stand up against him."

"You two have a little power," said the Mage, "but we will loan you some more. Let's all join hands. Science is learned, young man, so it won't make much difference to your power immediately, but it will reinforce what you already have. Young lady, Magic is feeling, and your powers will be boosted immediately. What's your name, by the way?"

"Kitty. Well, Catherine, really. We have powers? Really? Oh, I feel it! Can you feel it, Terry?"

He nodded. "It's a clarity and a sense of connectedness, but, sir, you've given me some power of feeling too. I can feel the cables in the walls and the power in them!"

The Mage nodded "There's always a crossover. No one is completely on the side of Science or of Magic. Learn to use your feelings, young man, and you, my dear, learn to use the clarity and sense of order that you'll get from your husband. Well, husband to be, that is."

"OK, let's get out of here. Stand clear, kids," said the Boffin, and blasted the door of the cell which fell to the floor in a tangle of bent metal.

"Are you a bit tetchy, dear? That was definitely over the top," said the Mage.

"Just a bit. I don't like being locked up, even though I could easily step out."

The Mage and the Boffin led Kitty and Terry up the stairs and towards the throne room. Two large men moved to stop them, but the Mage gestured and the guards froze in position, and the four of them entered the throne room.

Behind them, one of the large men found that he could talk.

"Can you move, Jones?" he asked.

"Only my head, Smith. You too?"

"Yes. I hope that this wears off soon. This is an uncomfortable position."

"Yeah, me too. When it wears off, let's walk out of here. I'm definitely not going to run. Definitely not."

"Is a fast walk OK by you?"

"Definitely."

In the throne room the Great Scientist turned in surprise.

"How did you get out? Oh, those kids must have let you out."

"It's over," said the Boffin. "You must step down immediately and leave the city."

"You dare..." said the Great Scientist, and pressed a button on his throne. A line of fire shot out and hit the Boffin, who staggered. A glow surrounded her.

"You're strong, aren't you?" she said. "Thank goodness for that little amulet."

The Mage sent a line of fire back at the Great Scientist, and a glow surrounded him as well. A stalemate developed with the Mage and the Boffin probing the Great Scientist's defences, and the Great Scientist probing back. Power beams and force fields rocked the room, and projectiles smashed windows and singed upholstery.

Kitty and Terry were ignored for the moment.

"Can you hit the red tile to the left of the throne, Kitty?" asked Terry.

Kitty formed a ball of fire and hurled it at the tile, and the air filled with the fragments. Terry dived forwards under the beams of power and pulled loose a bunch of cables which had been covered by the tile. The Great Scientist's weapons died.

"Nice move," said the Boffin approvingly.

The Great Scientist leapt from the throne and ran towards the door. He turned around, said "Vengeance!", pulled a gun and shot at the Boffin. The Mage stepped forward, plucked the bullet from the air and showed it to him. The Great Scientist disappeared through the doors.

"Nice going, kids. We would have beaten him eventually, because there are two of us, but that helped immensely, and reduced the amount of damage that would have occurred," said the Boffin as she held both of Kitty's hands. "Are you ready for the responsibility of your new roles?"

She briefly filled their minds with a feeling for what the jobs entailed, the responsibilities and the benefits. She reflected that she and the Mage had worked it out for themselves. Kitty looked at Terry, who put his arm around her.

Terry nodded. "Yes, we will do it. We're ready. But how do we start?"

"Well, firstly tell everyone. That you are the foci of the two powers. Draw in all the raw power of Magic and Science that is out there, and gather it to yourselves. Then you can start to work out how to undo the mess that the Great Scientist has left behind. You can't just shut the factories, as that will throw people out of work and created more chaos, but you can change what they make and how they are making it."

"I can put temporary filters on all the chimneys," said Terry.

"And we can make bricks and things, to fix up people's houses," said Kitty.

"Good ideas. But get some experts in. Get their opinions. I'm sure that there are good people out there. Is there anything else we can do before we go?"

"Go? Can't you stay for a while? Please!"

"We'll stay for a day or two, but you need to stand on your own two feet. Feel the needs. Work out the solutions."

They were still very young and lacking in confidence, and in the end the Mage and the Boffin stayed a week. Kitty and Terry opened up the Palace to everyone and everyone came. The Mage or the Boffin were always at their side and passed them occasional little notes like "waste of time" or "seems good value". People began calling Terry and Kitty "The Chief Scientist" and "The High Magician", and Terry and Kitty didn't deny it. Their confidence noticeably grew as time passed. They called back Smith and Jones to help control the crowds, and started to set up councils and committees. They delegated some tasks to others.

So the Mage and the Boffin were there at the end of the week when the Chief Scientist and the High Magician were married, surrounded by old friends and new. By chance, as they were exchanging vows in front of the celebrant, a hole appeared in the dark clouds and illuminated the open air setting that they had chosen. The Mage looked suspiciously at the Boffin, but she shook her head. It was natural. Pure chance.

When they took their leave Kitty hugged and kissed them both.

"What if we screw up? What can we do?" she asked.

The Boffin held both their hands and told them to step after her. They appeared in front of the Boffin's house.

"Welcome to our space. Welcome to our home."

"Is that your house? It's so nice!" said Kitty, and Terry nodded. Then they all stepped back again.

"Oh, that's so easy! I didn't know that we could do that."

"Yes, when we came here first we had to go by way of many other spaces, and that was not nice. Now we have been here once, it's so much easier. You're welcome at our place any time, but we may be away. If so, just drop a letter in the letter box, and we will know immediately, wherever we are. Oh, and one piece of advice. You should step down as rulers as soon as you can. Find a nice cottage like ours somewhere, where you can raise your children in peace. Only interfere if you have to, as interference often makes things worse."

Kitty looked at Terry. "We were saying the same thing earlier. Should we step down or do we need to be in charge? I'm glad that you mentioned that, as neither of us want to rule."

"You will still be important people, with a lot of influence. One more thing," said the Mage. "We have a space that we go to for a bit of peace and quiet. Our private space has no people but does have dragons. You should find your own quiet little retreat."

The Mage said privately to the Boffin later "I think that they will do well. There were plenty of good people that visited the Palace, all suppressed by the Great Scientist. I'm optimistic about this space. I think we'd better find out where the Great Scientist ran off to, though."

On a crag overlooking the city sat a man dressed in a tattered white coat. He'd lost his safety goggles and clipboard somewhere. Revenge and despair filled his mind. The Mage looked down on him from higher up the mountain and asked the Boffin "What are we going to do with him?"

"He's more pathetic than evil, isn't he?"

Suddenly the Great Scientist stood up, roared at the sky, and threw himself off the crag. The Mage and the Boffin both gasped and reached for him with all powers that they had, but to no avail. They stepped down to where his body had landed.

"What a sad end," said the Boffin.

"He had some powers after all. He fought us off all the way down. Maybe it was for the best, as I couldn't see him being happy anywhere."

The Mage and the Boffin had a few visits from Kitty and Terry in the early years, with the youngsters seeking advice. Mostly they just let the two young ones talk until they had worked out a solution for themselves. Sometimes they inserted a suggestion. They liked the two youngsters who reminded them of themselves when they were just starting out. Then Kitty and Terry starting bringing their children along, and the visits became more social than business.

The Mage and the Boffin visited their home space, and the changes were amazing. The dark dismal clouds were often replaced by fluffy white clouds in a blue sky. Even the grey rain clouds were an improvement. Terry, the Chief Scientist, had filters installed on the chimneys and developed a spray to remove most of the grime, and instead of dingy darkness, the brickwork on the house and other buildings was bright and gleaming. Many of the hovels had been replaced with functional, if not beautiful, state provided housing for those who needed it.

There was a long way to go, but Kitty, as High Magician, was pleased. Almost everyone approved of the changes, and the man in the street was happier and more optimistic than when the Great Scientist was in charge. People began to feel proud of the city, which, stripped of its grime, was a striking place. The harbour now looked appealing and people had taken to walking on the beaches and sailing yachts on the water. Unfortunately the water wasn't completely clean yet but it wouldn't be long before people were swimming in the blue-green waters.

"Do you think you have an answer to your question, dear?" the Mage asked the Boffin one day, after a visit from Kitty and Terry.

"You mean when I asked why we hadn't met ourselves?"

"Yes, that's what I meant."

"Mmm. Not really. Terry and Kitty remind me of us, but they aren't the same as us, are they?"

"They're really nice, but they're definitely different. The baby is cute, isn't she?"

"So is their little boy. He's, what, three?"

"Yeah, I almost feel like a grandfather. Yes, I know, I've been a grandfather so many times over the years."

"I know what you mean. But we've never met any Mage and Boffin close to us. Terry and Kitty are a long way away."

She sighed. "I guess we may never know. I'm not too unhappy about that. I think that it would be strange to meet myself."

***

Three Wishes

The Boffin and the Mage were browsing around their local market. They had picked up all the vegetables and other odds and ends that they needed and had arranged for eggs to be delivered and had ordered some bread. They had reached the section of the market that the Boffin thought of as the "Entertainment Section".

In this part of the market the travelling circuses and the sideshows were set up. Part of the reason that the Boffin liked to visit this section was to make sure that the scams were not too blatant and didn't separate the local citizens from too much of their money. A little money flowing from citizens pockets she considered reasonable, as it should teach them not to be too gullible, and the visitors needed to eat.

Partly she visited because now and then they came across someone in their line of business. A bush magician maybe, or a roving astronomer who would look the other way and cast horoscopes to earn his or her bread. Or a biologist with photographs and models of strange animals from distant parts, and maybe a cure for a crop disease. Then they would invite them home for a meal and a chat. They were generally interesting people.

On this occasion they came across a tent with a sign outside it that read "Three wishes, $150", and lounging outside was a turbaned man of more than average height, with glistening oiled muscles and a dark skin, darker even than the Boffin's. He had a beard and moustache, gold earrings and a gold chain and wore flowing robes which resembled the robes of an old time Eastlander. The Boffin couldn't put her finger on exactly why, but something about him whispered to her that he was the genuine article.

"$150 dollars for three wishes is expensive," the Boffin said to the turbaned man.

The Mage wandered over to see what his wife was doing.

"Well, if I put the price lower, people will buy the wishes, and I don't want them to do that."

"Why not," said the Mage.

"Well, I grant them their wishes, and they wish for silly things, or they accidentally wish for the wrong things, or they mess up the wishes in some other way, and then they get angry with me. Sometimes it's a real chore to sort things out."

He sighed.

"Why do you do it at all then?"

"I have to," he said and sighed. "Do you want to come in the tent and I'll explain. I can see that you are people of power. Maybe you will have some ideas."

He took down the sign and showed them in to his tent. There were three chairs in there and a small table with an ancient oil lamp, the sort made of brass and with a glass chimney. He poured them a strong coffee from a thermos flask.

"May I?" asked the Mage, indicating the lamp.

"Sure, but please don't rub it," said the turbaned man.

The Mage looked at lamp, but was careful not to rub it. It was inscribed with words of power, the sort that glow when you read them, but he didn't know the dialect. He put it down again.

"If you rub the lamp you will get three wishes," said the turbaned man. "I'm a Genie."

The Boffin said "I thought that it was something like that. Is it genuine, my dear?"

"Seems to be," said the Mage. "I can't read the words of power on his lamp, but it looks genuine. But I thought that wishing lamps were supposed to be those teapot shaped things?"

"We are trying to move with the times. Well, maybe catch up a bit. Maybe one day we will go electric. Who knows? People do so like old things."

"So, Mr Genie, what are you doing out of your lamp? I thought that someone had to rub it first to let you out, and then the wishes thing happens. Is that not the way it goes?"

"Please call me Mustapha. Well, I got fed up with the way that people kept messing up their wishes and blaming me, so I consulted the book, and found that there was no rule against me coming out of the lamp before it was rubbed. It's the action of rubbing the lamp that grants the wishes, and it is only tradition that it summons me too. I am tied to the lamp though, and have to come if it is rubbed, and I'm not already out."

"What book is that, Mustapha?" asked the Mage.

"'The Book of Rules and Regulations Pertaining to the Granting of Wishes on Rubbing a Magic Lamp'."

He gestured and an enormous book appeared on the table, causing it to creak under the strain. It almost knocked the lamp to the floor. The Mage grabbed it.

"That's the condensed version. The full version is nearly ten thousand pages long. Anyway, I discovered that I could come out of the lamp before anyone rubbed it. I tried warning people of the dangers of getting the wishes wrong, but they still did it and blamed me. I drew up a contract and got people to sign it, disavowing all responsibility, and they signed the contract and then screwed up their wishes and still blamed me. So I decided to charge them money to get their wishes, but they still did it, and still blamed me. So I put the price up really high and so far that has worked."

The Mage looked at the Boffin, and she nodded. "Mustapha, would like to come home with us? We can put you up for the night if you wish. We'd love to talk to you some more."

Mustapha smiled. "I'd love to," he said. "But my bed comes with me."

He gestured at the lamp. "Take me and the lamp home with you, and I'll invite you to visit **my** home."

"That's intriguing," said the Boffin.

So they drove home with the Genie in the back of the wagon alongside their shopping, cradling the lamp in his arms.

"How do you get about, Mustapha? Like this, carrying your home around with you?"

"Pretty much," said Mustapha. "Sometimes I pack it up and post it somewhere. Then I jump into it and travel inside it. I can step into it as long as it's reasonably close at the time. It's quite safe, and the lamp is much stronger than it looks. Thanks for catching it when I dropped the book on the table, but it wouldn't have come to any harm."

When they got to the Boffin and Mage's cottage the Genie put the lamp down on the table.

"I'll just be a minute," he said, and disappeared.

"Hmm," said the Boffin. "That's not a usual step. We usually step **across**. He stepped **in**."

Mustapha reappeared. "Folks, I'd like to welcome you to my home. Can we please hold hands? Now step with me."

The Boffin and the Mage stepped **in** with Mustapha and found themselves in a very pleasant modern sitting room. The furnishing did run a bit too much towards gold threading and heavy drapery, but the carpet was a stunning swirling mixture of browns, deep reds, bright yellows and blues, all surrounded by a square zigzag border.

"Oh, Mustapha, it's beautiful!" said the Boffin.

"Thank you. In some ways it leans towards the traditional, but we like it. Can I introduce my wife, Fee and my kids?"

Mustapha's wife and children came shyly in from the kitchen, and they all shook hands. Fee also bowed with her hand on her chest, and the Mage and the Boffin returned the salute.

There were three children and Fee carried a baby.

"The oldest girl is Fi, and the twin girls are Fau and Fum."

"And the baby?" asked the Boffin.

"He's not had a naming ceremony yet, but he will be called Ishmael."

"I'll show you round our house, and then we can eat," said Mustapha.

"I hope that you won't mind me mentioning it, Mustapha, but you don't seem to be, well, as muscly as you were when we met you at the market."

Mustapha laughed. "Oh yes, that's sort of like advertising. A Genie is supposed to be large and full of muscles, but most of us aren't naturally made that way."

Mustapha's house was roomy and very modern. The kitchen was light and airy and had a number of well-used gadgets.

"Fee's a marvellous cook," said Mustapha. "We trade her cakes and her sweetmeats with others and make quite a bit from them. Are the kids allowed a treat, Fee?"

Of course there was immediate clamouring for something from the kids. Fee sighed and doled out some sweet crispy biscuits from a tin. The Boffin and the Mage sampled them too. The Mage noticed that somehow the Boffin was now carrying the baby. He wasn't surprised, but he hadn't seen it happen. She loved babies and babies loved her.

"Show them your workshop, dear," said Fee, and Mustapha took them down a short corridor to his workshop.

It smelled of leather and wood and incense and glue. It seemed Mustapha worked mainly in wood, making chairs and stools with carved designs and mirror and picture frames also with elaborate designs carved into them. The style was distinctly Eastlander. He had cupboards and other furniture which he had made in the same style.

"We do well with Mustapha's carpentry too," said Fee. "It's a pity that we can't sell it 'up there'."

"Where you come from," clarified Mustapha. "If I carry stuff up there it just crumbles."

"What if it comes from 'up there' in the first place? Does it crumble after you've worked on it?"

Mustapha looked at Fee. "I've never tried that, have I? I wonder if that will work?"

Fee said "We'll have to try it. Have you seen the view from our garden?"

They all walked out into the garden and the Mage whistled. "Wow, that's different."

The vegetation was strange enough, with tall thick stalked plants with prickly bulbous flowers on the top, like a

176

pineapple on a stick, or a smooth stalked thistle. Smaller creeping plants with circular leaves stacked like plates covered the spaces between them. Trees abounded, tall and spreading and similar to trees "up there", but with a purple tinge to their trunks and foliage. Vines looped between the trees carrying great bulbous fruits of various colours like an unlit line of light bulbs.

In the actual garden, though Fee and Mustapha were growing plants that the Boffin recognised. Tomatoes, peppers, cucumbers. Various herbs in a square patch, and some sort of root vegetables further over.

The sky was totally different from "up there". It was all swirls of colours that slowly changed as the spirals rose and set. Small bright points, maybe moonlets or satellites rapidly crossed the horizon in mere minutes. Much further out than the swirls of colour and the racing moonlets but still close was a large orange red planet with rings like Saturn. It followed the sun as the two bodies crossed the sky in a stately place.

"Oh that's beautiful, Mustapha. Do you have stars at night?" asked the Mage.

"Yes, but not as many as 'up there'. I was so amazed by your night sky when I first went 'up there'. Here the night is rarely pitch dark as the Planet is often up in the sky, or the swirls of colour, which we call the High Winds, light things up."

"I notice that you grow vegetables from 'up there'. Is that for visitors?"

"No, I believe that we Genies, or Djinns, as we are sometimes called, originally came from 'up there', and we mostly eat food which comes from there. Some of the native stuff is edible, but it generally doesn't taste nice. Some does though. This herb is native. It's called 'Bitter Berry'."

Mustapha plucked two small fruits from a plant in the herb garden and gave then to the Mage and the Boffin.

"Mmm, a smokey flavour with a bit of a tang. Yes, that would make an interesting sauce," said the Boffin.

"Yes, and on that note, let us eat." Mustapha ushered them back into the house, and they sat down to eat.

Fee had prepared a table full of small dishes, cooked in the Eastlander style.

"Fee, this is marvellous!" said the Boffin, "I thought that I knew Eastlander style cookery, but there's so much here that I don't recognise. How did you cook this all so quickly?"

"Mustapha told me that you were coming when you left the market, and er, I used a little magic to help things along. You're not offended, are you? There are dishes there that have been forgotten in recent times. Recipes that come from my mother and Mustapha's mother."

"No, of course we aren't offended. We do that sometimes too," said the Boffin. "Oh, and are you offended by wine? If not, I'll step home to get a bottle."

"Sure," said Mustapha. "I don't drink, but Fee sometimes has a glass."

So the Boffin stepped back home and located the bottle of wine, and also a small block of wood. She stepped back into the lamp and presented the bottle of wine to Fee, who poured a glass for the three of them. Then they settled down to tasting Fee's cooking.

"Mmm, this is so good, Fee. I must get some recipes off you!"

"Thanks for the block of wood, Boffin. I know just what I want to carve in it." said Mustapha.

"You go and carve something, dear. I can see that you are itching to. We'll just carry on chatting," said Fee.

She served them strong dark coffee in small cups. The Boffin had somehow ended up with the baby again. The Mage himself was teaching Fi, Fau and Fum some simple conjuring tricks. Fi was guessing which hand the coin was hidden in almost all the time. The Mage frowned and cheated a little and Fi, laughing, still got it right. Hmm, some power there, thought the Mage.

"So, how far from the nearest town are you here, Fee?" asked the Boffin.

"We don't have any towns as such," said Fee. "We're very spread out. Somebody has something to sell, they put the word out, we all turn up and put up our tents in a field and bring our stuff to trade. At one time we didn't have permanent homes, but these days we have mostly settled down."

She thought a bit. "Maybe we will start to build towns as the population grows. Our nearest neighbour is a lot closer than he used to be. But many of us like our temporary tent markets."

"How do you keep in touch, Fee. You're pretty isolated here."

Fee laughed. "Oh, we use globes, which are not unknown 'up there', are they?"

The Boffin nodded. "Yes, but not everyone uses them. How do you get around? There don't seem to be any roads."

"By carpet." Fee indicated the marvellous carpet under their feet. "Those are also known 'up there', aren't they?"

"Yes, but they are rare. So rare that most people, including me, thought that they were mythical. Fancy that!"

"Oh, I didn't know that. I've not been 'up there' very much since we had the kids. It's a strange space, isn't it? Oh, but not for you, I forgot. I'm sorry."

"That's OK. It's sometimes strange for us too!" The Boffin laughed.

Mustapha came back just as they were talking about the differences between the two spaces. "We ought to spend more time up there, Fee. There so much to learn there. Most of the advances in our space have come from there, one way or another. Our kitchen. Our bathroom! My tools in my workshop. Some of our medicines. Our people originally came from there, of course."

"Your space is lovely, Mustapha. But it doesn't yet have schools and universities," said the Mage. "I think that you will do, in the future. I hope that you are able to import the good things like schools and universities and not the bad things, like pollution and poverty. By the way, if you want to visit, you and your kids are welcome to stay with us if you want."

Mustapha smiled. "Thank you for the offer, but we are by nature travellers. The lamp gives us a place to stay, wherever we are, 'up there'. But we'll definitely visit, if we can. If we send the kids up there to school or even university, we may take you up on that offer."

He continued "I was wondering if you had any solution to our problem of the lamp, though. You are people with power. I can tell that."

"You have your own powers," said the Mage. "Fee casually mentioned using magic to help things along when she was cooking. Little Fi has quite strong powers, I noticed. We are not well versed in your types of powers, but maybe we can advise you. Is there anything in the rules that says that the lamp must be a certain shape and size?"

"No, nothing, except that it must be capable of giving light, and it must be made of brass. The original lamps were brass, of course."

The Mage clicked his fingers and said "What about this?"

He held a brass filigree case, shaped like a heart and hanging from a necklace chain. He pressed a button on the side and the top opened, revealing a knurled wheel. He flicked it and a spark from a flint set light to a wick dipped in fuel. It was a delicate little lighter.

"You can make it look like that?" asked Mustapha. "But what happens when I go into it? In the past the wrong people have found it, and silly things happen. They wish that they are wealthy and then find that it doesn't make them happy, or they lose it all. Or they wish for a beautiful wife, and she turns out to be vain and a nag. Something like that always seems to happen. Most often the third wish is to return things to the way they were."

"Well, you can put it in a safe place, like deposit box in a bank, or something like that. You could hang it around your neck! It's not a perfect solution of course. You told us a story of a genie who hid his lamp in a cave protected by a spell, and it still was found, wasn't it? That's just an early version of the deposit box. I can give you a charm to hide it, but it won't be completely unfindable. Meanwhile, I'll research the lamps. I have a friend who is an expert on Eastlander spells and charms. I'll give you his address."

Mustapha nodded. "Thank you for that. I'll go and visit him. As far as keeping the lamp safe, that's about what I've been doing. I've been hiding it, but now and then someone finds it. I can't create a charm to hide it, because of the rules, but I didn't think of getting someone else to do it. That's double protection, isn't it?"

The Mage said "Someone must have created the lamps, and there must be a way to alter how they work. I think that because of the way that the wisher usually ends up worse off than before he or she made the wishes, that the creator was very upset about something. I'm just sorry that we can't be more help."

"Thank you, Mage, and you too, Boffin, for all your help," said Mustapha. "It's been great to be able to talk these things over with someone who understands the problems that we are having. People with power like you are rare."

"Anyway," he continued, "please tell me what you think of this."

He passed the carved piece of wood to the Boffin. She gasped.

"Oh, that's amazing," she said. "Look, dear."

She passed the piece of wood to the Mage. He saw an intricate carving of the likenesses of himself and the Boffin in bas-relief. His likeness held a stylised flame in the palm of his hand, while the Boffin held a pair of dividers and was measuring a globe.

"Oh my goodness," he said. "This is your test piece to see if it crumbles 'up there'? It's almost too good to risk! If this survives, may we keep it?"

"I carved it for you," said Mustapha. "To thank you for your help and for visiting us. We don't get many visitors from 'up there', and we really appreciate it."

"Well, we'd best be going," said the Mage, "if you can pry the baby away from the Boffin. Please all come to breakfast in the morning. We'll cook pancakes."

Little Fi's eyes widened and her mouth opened.

"Please can we go, Dad?" she asked.

Mustapha looked at Fee.

"That's should be OK," she said. "We'll knock on the front door though when we come. You don't want people suddenly appearing in the middle of your kitchen!"

"Are you coming with us, Mustapha, to see how your carving fares?" said the Mage.

The three of them stepped up to the Mage and Boffin's house, the Mage carrying the carving.

"How long does it take to crumble, Mustapha?" he asked.

"Almost immediately," said Mustapha. "It looks like the trick worked. I'll have to start importing timber down home. I'm kicking myself for not thinking of it before. Thank you for the idea, and thank you for inviting us for breakfast. It will be the first time that we've brought the kids up here. They're going to be so excited. I'd better go and help Fee calm them down. Goodnight."

He disappeared.

"Nice people," said the Mage.

"Very nice. I don't think that we've met a Djinn before, have we?"

"No, I don't believe we have. I was surprised when he stepped **in**, weren't you?"

"Yes, I was. But I thought afterwards that we do know something about the microscopic levels, electrons and protons, and all the other particles. I don't know how that relates to Mustapha's space, but my guess is that it does. Hmm."

The Mage knew that the Boffin would be pondering what she had learned for months or years, and possibly doing some experiments. It was part of her nature. He himself would be doing his own thinking and research in his own way. The old books. Similar spells. And he would likely do some experiments too. His sort of experiments.

Some months later the Mage got a letter from his friend, the one who was interested in Eastlander spells and charms. He told the Boffin about it.

"It seems that Han and Mustapha have been able to modify the spell on the lamps. Hmm, he calls it a charm. Anyway, Han tells me that the charm I put on the lamps to deter people is working and Mustapha reports that no one has rubbed his lamp in ages. But more importantly, they've managed to 'switch off' the wish charm, so that rubbing the lamp has no effect. Mustapha says that some of his people don't want to switch off the charm, so it's good that the charm has to be modified lamp by lamp."

"That's great, dear. Does Han say anything about Mustapha's carpentry business?"

"Yes, apparently Mustapha's carving are fetching high prices. He still makes furniture, but gets more for carvings like the one he did for us."

They both looked at the carving, which the Boffin had mounted on the wall.

"Han says that Fee sends her love, and so do the kids. Apparently Fee's kids and Han's kids were running riot, while he was writing. They all seem to be having great fun. Fee and Mustapha often bring the kids up here now."

"I must ask them all to stay soon," said the Boffin. "It's a good thing Fee and I swapped charms so that we could keep in touch."

"A charm? You?"

"Yes, one of the first that you taught me, so long ago, my dear. Is that so surprising? Scientists always cross their fingers before they perform an experiment. Didn't you know?"

***

The Duplicated Man

One summer evening the Boffin and the Mage were sitting outside enjoying the sunset when a young man came up the drive. He passed through the Boffin's detectors and the charms and spells of the Mage let him through, so he didn't appear to be dangerous. They watched him approach with interest.

"Good evening," he said. "Am I correct in assuming that you are the Boffin and the Mage of this space?"

The Boffin and the Mage knew what he meant when he referred to 'this space'. Another name that they sometimes used for the same thing was 'this Universe'. The Mage and the Boffin knew that their space or Universe was surrounded by other spaces or Universes that had at some time in the past split from their space or Universe. The Boffin's students, annoyingly she thought, liked to refer to this theory as the parallel or alternative world theory.

So, their visitor was claiming to come from another space or Universe. Since the Mage and the Boffin frequently visited other spaces or Universes by 'stepping' to them, they knew that it was possible.

"Yes, we are," said the Mage. "Can we help you?"

The young man sagged. "Oh, I hope so, I really hope so. May I sit down? I've travelled a long way and stepped through many worlds, some of them nowhere near as nice as this one."

"Come on into the house," said the Boffin. "We were about to go in anyway."

The Boffin led him to the kitchen, which is the room that they used most of the time when the Boffin wasn't in her laboratory and the Mage wasn't in his study.

"Would you like some tea? And maybe one of the Boffin's cakes?" asked the Mage. "Then you can tell us your story. What's your name, by the way, and where do you come from?"

"My name is Thomas. Tom for short. I come from a space quite a long way away, over there." He gestured.

"Ah. Did you pass through a space where Kitty and Terry are the foci of Science and Magic."

Tom nodded. "Yes, and they recommended that I search you out, and, by the way, they sent their regards and said that they were going to visit soon."

"Oh good. They're nice people and so are their kids."

The stranger nodded. "Yes, very. They tried to help me with my problem, but we ran out of options after a while. So they suggested that I should seek you out. They were very busy at the time with the elections. People insisted on consulting them, they said. Terry said 'It isn't hard work, but we have to do it. Almost all the time it consists of just listening, then letting people make up their own minds. For some reason people think that you are wise when you do that. We interfere as little as possible and the difficult part is to convince people that we don't support any particular option. The Mage and the Boffin taught us that.'."

"Yeah, we had to work it out for ourselves," said the Mage. "We could have saved a lot of heartache if we had realised it earlier. Anyway, Tom, tell us about yourself. What is your problem?"

"Well, how old do you think I am?" asked Tom.

The Boffin ran an instrument over him.

"Good gracious! According to this, you are three years old. But you look, what, twenty-five, twenty-six? Can you explain this?"

Tom sighed. "Yes, that is exactly my problem. I was born twenty-six years ago into a loving family. My father is a banker and my mother is a teacher. My parents named me Rhys, a family name, and I have an older brother and a younger sister. I did well in science at school, and my parents sent me to Central University where I studied physics."

The Mage glanced at the Boffin. "They named you Rhys? But why do you call yourself Tom?"

"I'll come to that later," said Tom.

He continued. "I gained my degree, and stayed on to do research. We were studying matter transfer, under the direction of a professor of the school. We, that is Gareth and I, wanted to be able to transport people from, say, the Earth to the Moon. You do have a Moon here, don't you?" he asked, suddenly worried.

"Oh dear. Matter transfer," said the Boffin. "Yes, we do have a Moon. Most human spaces seem to have at least one large Moon."

Tom looked at the Boffin. "You know about matter transfer?"

"Well, only in theory. Matter transfer operates at a level below the normal macroscopic level. We call it the quantum level, and it's a level governed by probability, roughly speaking. Pretty much anything can happen, but usually doesn't. Roughly speaking. Generally it's easier to move things from one place to another the usual ways than to use matter transmission."

"Anything can happen, as you say, but usually doesn't. Sometimes it does, though," said Tom, nodding. "And that's my problem."

"We had built a machine, Gareth and I," he continued. "We'd transmitted blocks of various elements and simple compounds from one station to the other, and they had disappeared from the one station and appeared, unchanged so far as we could tell, in the other. So we sent bacteria. They seemed fine. We sent guinea pigs. They appeared unharmed. So we decided to go for the big one. We drew lots to see who would be the first human to be transferred. I won, or lost, depending on how you look at it."

"Did you have no failures?" asked the Boffin.

"None at all. If we had we wouldn't have tried the human transfer. But we were so keen to make history, and, ironically, that's what we did."

The Boffin nodded. "Go on."

"So I stepped onto the transfer plate. I was feeling great. I had no qualms whatsoever. I gave Gareth the thumbs up, and he hit the switch."

"What did you feel?" asked the Boffin.

"Well, nothing. One instant I was on one side of the lab, standing on the plate, and the next I was on the other side of the lab, standing on the other plate."

"I'm guessing something went wrong," said the Mage.

"So, I'm sort of getting ready to cheer, but Gareth was looking at the other transfer plate and saying 'Oh darn, what went wrong' and I saw myself step off the sending plate."

"Ah. So your machine duplicated you instead of transferring you?" said the Mage.

"Yeah, and all hell broke loose. There was two of me. I remembered appearing on the receiving plate, but he didn't. For that reason Gareth and the other me reasoned that he was the real me."

"What happened then?"

"Well, we stopped the experiments of course. The University wouldn't have let us continue anyway. Then there was a big discussion of what this all meant. And finally we all decided to leave it for the night. I and my duplicate went to our car and had a bit of a discussion about whose car it was and who should drive. I let him drive. When we got home, he said that he would make the guest bed up for me. I was outraged at first, but I gave in. My mind was telling me that he was the 'original' me, and that I was a duplicate."

He sighed. "Then the trouble started. Every time that anyone spoke to 'Rhys' both of us would answer. So we decided that I should be called Thomas, which was our middle name. Tom for short, of course. But as far as the authorities were concerned, I didn't exist. I wasn't born, I didn't go to school, I didn't have a flat, I didn't have a job, and what is more, I didn't have any money."

"Oh, Rhys helped out, of course, since he essentially was me and could understand my situation. He was closer to me than a brother. We argued with the University that they had a responsibility to me, since the experiment was sanctioned by them, and so they offered me a job. But it took a long time to convince them."

"Then of course, I needed ID. So we went to the authorities, who proved to be a much harder nut to crack. Well, our story was incredible, wasn't it. They needed proof, which of course we didn't have. Only the logs of our experiment. In the end they settled for a signed and authenticated letter from our Professor, and I got my ID, but it was only a temporary one. So Tom now officially sort of existed."

"With my ID, I could get a bank account, driver licence, and all those things that one needs to get by these days. I started back at the University and life started to return almost to normal. People at the University used to think that we were twins. At least, those who didn't know what had happened did."

"Our co-workers acted a bit odd around us. They talked to Rhys and pretty much ignored me. As one girl said, apologetically, 'You're not the real Rhys, are you?'."

"In the end, I'd had enough and decided on a fresh start. I saw an advert for a job at Southern University and decided to apply. I told Rhys, and he laughed and showed me an advert for a job at Northern University. 'Let's put the whole country between us, eh?' he said. So we did."

Tom paused. "Did I mention my family? I don't think I did, did I? They were, obviously, shocked by the whole thing, but they eventually took it in their stride. Mum even claimed to be able to tell us apart, but she was just kidding herself. My sister said that she wished that she had a duplicate, so that they could share homework and things like that. My brother wasn't there. His Army unit was off somewhere rebuilding a bridge that had been damaged in floods, but he sent his love and his hope that we'd be able to fix things."

"Anyway, we showed them the job adverts, and Mum, of course, didn't want us to go so far away. Dad however nodded his head. He could see that we needed space to grow apart. So

I headed south and Rhys headed north, and after that we only saw each other every few months."

"It sounds like you made the best of a bad thing," said the Boffin. "But what happened next? What caused you to step so far from home?"

"I was just getting to that. One day Rhys phoned me. 'Are you going to go home for Sissy's birthday?' he asked. 'I'm bringing someone that I want you all to meet.'. I hadn't been meaning to, but he was so mysterious, and wouldn't say any more, so I booked my flight the same day. As it happens I arrived earlier than Rhys and found out that Mum, Dad, and Sissy had no idea what Rhys was up to either. So Dad and I drove back to the airport to pick up Rhys and his friend."

"Rhys came down the tunnel holding hands with a girl. My heart leapt when I saw her, and I knew. I knew we were in trouble. I knew without a shadow of a doubt that Rhys had fallen in love with her and was going to announce their engagement."

"I see where this is headed," said the Mage. "You, of course, also fell in love with her as you and Rhys are, to all extents and purposes, the same person. Oh dear."

"Yes, exactly. That weekend was terrible. Rhys did announce their engagement, and we all congratulated them. Milly, that was her name by the way, was so happy, but when she was introduced to me, she was puzzled. I cornered Rhys when she wasn't around and found that he hadn't told her about me. All he had told her was that I was his twin! At first, I was annoyed, then I realised that I would probably have done the same, if things had been the other way around."

"Did he tell her?" asked the Mage.

"Yes, eventually. After we had spent most of the weekend with her calling me Rhys and calling Rhys Tom. It was when she tried to kiss me, thinking that I was Rhys, and I refused, though I obviously wanted to, that she realised that something was wrong. So we three sat down and Rhys told her about my origins. Of course, she then remembered that we had been in the news."

"How did she take it?" asked the Boffin.

"Very well. She looked at me and said 'You love me too, don't you?'. I said 'Yes, of course. But I won't cause any trouble, I assure you. I want you to be happy. Both of you.' She thought a bit and said 'Will that be enough?'."

"Was she right? Was that enough? I suspect not, because here you are, wandering through the spaces, looking for an answer," said the Boffin.

"I tried hard. I really did. I stayed away from them as much as I could. I only went to family gatherings if I had to, and I spent a lot of time and effort dating other girls. None of it worked. I came to hate the other me, the original. Though I didn't really, of course. I had fantasies where he died. Then I regretted my thoughts. I pretended that I hated Milly, but of course I didn't. I contemplated suicide. I regularly got drunk. I didn't resort to drugs, but I considered it. I was, frankly, a mess. The last straw was the wedding."

"Ah, that must have been hard."

"Yes. The silly thing was that I sincerely wished them well. I wanted Milly to be happy, and my other self too. He was or rather is me, after all. Well, I went to the wedding. I saw them happily married, and the only cloud was me. I decided that something needed to happen and soon, and the funny thing was, so did they. They dragged me aside at the party after the wedding. 'We think that you need to do something, Tom,' said Rhys. 'You are cracking up before our eyes. So we think that you ought to go and see our friend, Sandra. She's a psychiatrist, but that's only one part of her skills. If you consult her, she may be able to help you.'."

"What did you think of that? Had you consulted any doctors about this before they suggested it?"

"Funnily enough, no. It sort of seemed like admitting defeat. 'Promise me you will go and see her,' said Milly. Then she kissed me. Not a simple peck on the cheek, but a full-blown mouth-to-mouth, breath destroying kiss. 'I promise,' I said, somewhat stunned. Rhys clapped me on the back, and smiled. I'm pretty sure they'd talked it out beforehand."

"Milly, and for that matter, your other self, seem to be smart people. Did you go and see the psychiatrist?" asked the Boffin.

"Yes, with mixed feelings. I didn't think I was nuts, but I was a bit frazzled. Sandra was a clever person, and made some helpful suggestions. She knew about me of course from the news and of course, Rhys and Milly had told her about me as well. It was such a comfort to tell someone, other than Rhys and Milly, about my problems and Sandra really listened. I was feeling positive for the first time. I could handle this! I told Sandra, but Sandra said 'Well, any improvement is likely to be only temporary. Every time you see Rhys and Milly it will be like a slap in the face.' She was just being realistic."

The Mage nodded. "Yes, she was right. Twins sometimes suffer from this sort of envy. But did she propose any solution?"

"Yes, she did. She knew of my work, well, our work, and she knew about other spaces, though the current jargon is 'alternative universes', I believe."

He hesitated. "I don't think that Sandra was a focus for Science or Magic, like you are, but she knew about stepping. She showed me how to step to other spaces. I was amazed. I was a scientist, but there were whole new spaces out there, which science, our science, knew nothing about, except theoretically."

"Yes, People in Science dominated spaces tend to forget how to step quite early on in human development. Any sentient being and quite a few semi-sentient beings can step. It's just that humans have forgotten how to do it," said the Boffin. "So, she showed you how to step. Did she have a reason to show you?"

"Yes, she thought that it should be simple to find a space where there was no Rhys, but there was a Milly. Then I could move into that space, and Milly would fall in love with me. It turned out that it wasn't that simple. It seemed that where there was no Rhys, there was no Milly either. I don't know why, and neither did Sandra."

"That's interesting," said the Boffin looking at the Mage. "We've thought about this a bit, haven't we, dear?"

The Mage looked thoughtful. "Yes, We've noticed that some people form strong bonds. Like Kitty and Terry. The Boffin and me. And, it seems, Rhys and Milly. Other people form bonds which are not as strong, or maybe just different. Like Rose, who has been happily married twice. Or Leon, who hasn't been married and seems quite happy with the situation. Maybe those who form really strong bonds can't exist in spaces where the other partner does not exist. It's just a guess."

"Yes, but we don't really know if it is true or not. It sounds possible though," said the Boffin. "So, Tom, what happened then? You've been roaming the spaces, maybe looking for the impossible, and eventually you've wound up here?"

"Pretty much," said Tom. "I quickly discovered that in some spaces, certain people were the centres of power, of the forces of Science and Magic. Most often there were two of them, but sometimes there was only one, and occasionally the powers were spread over several people. Then I stumbled on the space where Kitty and Terry were the foci. They were kind enough to try to help me, but when they couldn't, they recommended that I try to find you. They said that you were the most powerful people that they knew. They described you as the archetypes, but I don't know what that means."

"That sort of means 'the originals from which others are made'," said the Boffin. She looked at the Mage. "We're definitely not the originals, but we are closer to them than most. We did have predecessors."

"Do you think you can help me?" asked Tom, desperately.

"We'll do our best. But let's sleep on it. I've got some ideas, but we'll have clearer heads in the morning."

So they all retired for the night. In the morning the Boffin and Tom quickly disappeared into the Boffin's laboratory. The Mage dropped in on them, but they were busy scrawling equations and bullet points and diagrams on the Boffin's whiteboard and computers, so the Mage smiled, made them some coffee, and left them to it. He retired to his study to consult his books of lore and his grimoires. Then he cast a few searching spells, researched his books again, consulted his crystal ball and generally investigated in his own way. But he already had some ideas.

He made them omelettes for lunch and dragged them out of the laboratory and made them sit down and eat.

"Any luck?" he asked.

"Well," the Boffin said, "we've found the errors in the original field equations, and we've pretty much patched up them so that they more accurately represent what happened. We believe that there was a one in ten chance that the duplication happened, and we can reduce that to one in ten thousand. We're confident that we can reduce it to one in ten million or so fairly easily, and..."

"How does that help?" interjected the Mage.

The Boffin and Tom looked at each other. "Well if we can understand what happened..."

"Then you can stop it happening again. But it has already happened. What about that?"

The Boffin said "You are right, dear. We haven't been addressing the real problem. Do you have any ideas?"

"Oh, I'm working on a few things," said the Mage and sauntered off.

The Boffin watched him go. "He's up to something," she said.

She turned to Tom and said "Right, let's reconsider our approach...."

At the end of the week the Boffin and Tom were looking glum.

"Well, at least we've made some advances in the science," said the Boffin. "Those may be useful in the future, but as for your problem, Tom, we've not been able to make any progress."

"Where's the Mage?" asked Tom. "Has he made any progress?"

"Huh, he'd not tell me until he was sure. He's gone off to town for something, and he wouldn't say what. He's being annoying."

Just then the front door opened, and the Mage called out. "I'm back! And I've someone here I'd like you to meet."

He walked into the kitchen, where the Boffin and Tom were drinking coffee. Following him was a young lady. Tom started.

"Milly? Milly, what are you doing here?" he asked.

"Hi, I'm Lilly," said the girl. "You must be Tom. I'm pleased to meet you."

"L-lilly? You're not Milly?"

She shook her head. "No, I'm not. In the same way that you are not Rhys."

The Mage tried to pour himself some coffee, and found that only a dribble was left. "Huh! You could have topped it up. Scientists!"

The Boffin took the coffee jug from the Mage and went to make some more. "Why don't you tell the story from the beginning, Lilly? I bet it's a fascinating tale."

"Oh, OK," said Lilly. "It all started while I was studying at Central University. It had the best school of Magic, and I didn't mind moving down from the north."

"That's odd. Northern had the best school of Magic where I come from," said Tom.

"Yes, so the Mage told me. He's told me all about you." She blushed a little.

She continued. "Anyway, it was there that I met my boyfriend, Rhys. Yes, I know that is your original name, Tom.

We were going out with each other for about six months and were thinking of getting engaged. He told me about their experiment, and I was really interested. In the Magic school, we'd been trying to do much the same, though we were trying to use it to move large objects around. We called it a 'lifter' and we were getting somewhere, but the boys and girls in the Science school seemed to be further on than we were."

"There was always rivalry between the Magic and Science schools, but it was friendly rivalry. We often swapped insights, and Rhys offered to show me their experimental setup. So I visited Gareth and Rhys in the lab one day and watched them move blocks of metal and wood from one station to the other. They were ecstatic. They sent some microbes from one station to the other, and tried it with some rabbits and it worked."

"We used guinea pigs," said Tom.

"Then they looked at each other and said 'What about a human?' They discussed the risks and so on for a while, but I knew they were going to do it. 'Who then?' said Gareth and looked at me. Rhys immediately objected, but Gareth pointed out that it needed both of them to do the transfer."

"That's funny. We only needed one. Oh, but if we hadn't picked up that stabiliser circuit, we would have needed two," said Tom.

Lilly continued. "Well, in the end, we all agreed that I would be the first person to be transferred. I remember Rhys said 'This will make you famous.' He wasn't wrong! I stood on the plate and watched as Rhys and Gareth operated the machine. I suddenly found myself on the other plate, and I was just about to cheer when Rhys said 'What went wrong? There was a power surge, but she didn't go.' That's when Milly stepped off the sending plate. She saw me at the same time as I saw her, and we both shrieked. Then everything went crazy."

She looked at Tom. "You know what happened then, don't you, Tom? We were front page news for a few days, but then some politician got caught embezzling money, and it sort of faded away. But there I was, with no identity, with a boyfriend who now suddenly had two identical girlfriends. Well, the school of Science did their best to help, helping me with sorting out my ID problems and the school of Magic offered me a job. It was fine for a while, but Rhys kept mistaking me for Milly and vice versa, and it was plainly not working."

"Finally Milly, Rhys, and I had a talk. We decided, well, I decided really, that I should get out of the situation and I transferred to Southern. It was down there that I met Sandra, who was working as a counsellor and therapist. She introduced me to stepping and suggested that I look for a space with a Rhys but not a Milly. Well, I knew about stepping in theory, and I knew that some people did it, but I hadn't thought that it could help me. I couldn't find any spaces with just a Rhys but then I finally got lucky!"

"Let me guess," said Tom. "You met Kitty and Terry?"

"Oh yes! They are lovely people, and their kids are lovely too. They told me about you, Tom, and I realised that I needed to find you."

"We think that couples who have a strong bond like Rhys and Milly are never found alone, across all the spaces. That's what makes your situation so tragic, you two," said the Boffin. "But you eventually met Terry and Kitty."

"Yes, I was just about giving up, and they gave me the strength to carry on, so I stepped this way until I got here. I visited the Mage's old friend in the school of Magic at Central University, and you know the rest."

"We don't," said the Boffin, looking crossly at the Mage who was trying not to smile.

"My friend listened to Lilly's story," said the Mage, "and contacted me. He put her on a plane to here and I picked her up at the airport. And that is how she got here."

"Hmm," said the Boffin suspiciously. She would have a word with the Mage later.

Later on, the Boffin suggested that the two young people take a walk down to the lake. They accepted with such alacrity that it was obvious that they both been trying to figure out a polite way to be alone together. She watched them until they were out of sight, but they were hand in hand well before that. The Mage came and stood beside her.

"They'll be OK," he said. "After all, they are just correcting an anomaly."

"Yes, dear. Do you think that there are any more Lillys or Toms out there?"

"It's very unlikely." He showed her his crystal ball. He knew that she was adept at reading it.

"Oh yes. I see. That conjunction of lines fades to nothing there, and that other group of lines joins it. It's a definite zero in my terms. Ah, that agrees with our equations too! We couldn't see why we were getting nulls all over the place. That explains it!"

She turned to him. "Right, now explain yourself?"

"Explain what, my dear?" he said innocently.

"You know. How did you get her here, and how did you know she even existed?"

"Ah, that. Well, like I said, he was an anomaly, and the space he was in couldn't autocorrect itself because there was already a Rhys and a Milly there. So another space nearby introduced the correction, Lilly. Of course it was a space with a Rhys and a Milly. Now they are together there is no anomaly. A bit of a tangle in the spaces maybe, but no anomaly."

"I guessed that there had to be a Lilly," he continued, "but I didn't know for sure. But there were an infinite number of spaces with Milly and Rhys in them, and only one with a Lily in it as well, if she existed. No wonder they couldn't find each other. I also guessed that Sandra or Sandra-like people might exist in multiple spaces. The ones that step often do, so I sort of sent a broadcast to all the Sandra-like people to look out for a Lilly and direct her our way. Once they were away from the 'Milly and Rhys' spaces, it was almost certain that they would find each other."

"Smart ass," said the Boffin lovingly. "You'll have to show me how you did that some time. I suppose the Sandras didn't realise that they had received a message? It would be like a feeling or intuition, right? So how did you know Lilly had arrived here? Oh, you warned your friend in Central that she might appear looking for us."

"Exactly. I think my approach won out this time," he said smugly.

"Yes," she said grudgingly, "I suppose. We'll have to find them a nice space with no Rhys and Milly in it. That shouldn't be too hard. Tom's a pretty good scientist. What about Lilly?"

"Yes, she'll do well in my field. She's got the intuition and the empathy."

He sighed and put his arm round his wife. "Another happy ending. Another problem solved."

She kissed him. "That's what we are here for, after all."

***

Together

"I wonder about you and me, sometimes," said the Mage one day.

The Boffin considered. They'd been together so long that they might only speak a dozen or so words to each other in a day. They knew each other so well that they didn't need any more than that to communicate their wants and needs and, more importantly, to express their affection and love for one another.

So the Mage was not talking about them as people, as husband and wife, but about their roles as "Mage" and "Boffin". She was aware that she often did things which were, strictly speaking, not part of her role as the supposedly scientific "Boffin". But the Mage himself wasn't shy of using scientific and mathematical methods, especially statistics. He was very good at statistics.

"We've never been stuffy about our roles, have we?" she said.

"Mmmm. But you're very protective of our kids. That's an emotional trait."

"I don't deny it. But you flattened the walls around that town when the King captured our daughter. You broke into the dungeons to get to our sons when they were imprisoned by that other King. You practically stormed the school when that girl was bullying our other daughter. You..."

"OK, OK. You've made your point. Parental feelings don't count with respect to our roles!"

They were silent for a while.

"You are wondering if we will end up so similar that for all practical purposes, so far as our roles are concerned anyway, that there will be little point in saying that I'm the Boffin and you're the Mage? Hmmm."

She came and sat next to him on the sofa. He put his arm around her, and she curled her feet up on the seat and leant against him.

"My analysis is that our empathy for the other point of view was one of the reasons that we were chosen, all that time ago. Possibly the main reason. Everything is interconnected, I say, and I know you agree. You might call it magic and I might call it science, but there's really little difference. You say magic is about feelings, but you are one of the most logical people I know. And science is about logic, but you know what happens when one of my experiments doesn't produce the result I expect?"

"Yep, you sulk for a day or two."

"I do not sulk! I merely spend a day or two reviewing the experiment and considering the possible reasons for its failure."

"You sulk."

"I wouldn't call it sulking. I'm not happy though. Anyway, we look at things from different directions but come to much the same conclusions. We'll never change our fundamental ways of looking at things. But we might borrow things from each other's way of working. You did a nice analysis of the poison that the crazy man tried to use on the Prince, by the way. That's an example of what I am talking about."

"Thank you. Though it's not nice to call the poor man 'crazy'."

She acknowledged his point.

"Yeah, you're right, of course. At least now he's got someone to look after him, and the charms and the medicine should help him out."

She turned to him. "So what do you think, my dear? Are we turning into each other? A Boffin-Mage or a Mage-Boffin? What do you feel?"

"I think that we should exclude the parental emotions from consideration. Everyone has those as you pointed out. See, I'm analysing things like a Boffin! Also things move from the realm of magic to the realm of science all the time, but the realm of magic doesn't shrink. What is an atom but a little bundle of magic, after all? Most people don't know or understand the science of it. Feelings and intuitions are still my way of looking at the world, but, even before we met, I would always double check with logic and reason. I think that everyone is part Mage and part Boffin, and we are no different. We'll never have the same world view, and we'll never merge our roles."

He kissed her and she kissed him back. Somehow this was a confirmation and resolution of their discussion.

"So, why the question?" she asked.

"There's something in the air that I can't put my finger on."

He emphasised this by creating a small circle of light in the air with his finger. The Boffin gestured at it and it floated over to her. She stretched it and positioned it over her head.

The Mage laughed. "A halo?"

He gestured and was sitting with his arm around a small devil, complete with horns and tail. The halo looked incongruous.

"Huh," she said and became herself again. She waved the halo out of existence.

"Let me see," she said pulling an instrument out of her pocket. She projected the readings on to the wall so that they both could have a look.

"Nothing is registering. Well, there's low level disturbances, but that's fairly normal. Quantum. Oh, and it's going to rain tomorrow. Can you see anything?"

"I agree. Nothing. There's a little bit of a control struggle, down on the right there, but that's likely to be local politics, I think. Nothing serious."

She could tell he was frustrated by his feeling that something was not right. "You know I trust your feelings, dear. Let's just keep an eye on things for a while. It might be something just below the level of the physical, and it might disperse in a day or two, or it might become clearer."

He knew she was trying to ease his frustration, so he kissed her. "Yes, let's do that."

She was projecting the readings onto the wall of her laboratory a couple of days later when the Mage came in. She noticed him coming and held out her hand to him, and he took it.

"You were right, my love. I still don't see anything specific, but something is definitely going on. Those low level disturbances are increasing. The whole display is varying from green to yellow. If I focus on a small area I don't get any detail. Do you get anything with your charms and spells?"

"No, but it's across spaces, I think. What do your instruments say about that?"

She frowned and tapped some commands into her computer. The screen cleared and was replaced by single wave which slowly waxed and waned.

"That's odd. It is across spaces but I can't tell the direction. I thought I'd fixed that problem."

"I think the effect is increasing, whatever it is," said the Mage.

"Is there anything we can do?" asked the Boffin.

"Polish up our spells and charms? Dust off our equations?"

He put his arm around her. "We don't know what direction the threat, if it is a threat, is coming from. We don't know what the threat even is, if it is a threat. We have our amulets, powered by your science and protected by my magic. There's something about this that is disturbing you, isn't there?"

"It's the fact that we can't get a hold on whatever it is. It's all so vague.

Just then there was a tentative knock on the door, and the Boffin's screen went red.

The Mage smiled and said "Showtime! It looks like we are about to find out."

He kissed his wife to reassure her, and they went to open the door. Outside were a young boy and girl in their early teens. They were shabbily dressed in clothes that were meant for people much bigger than they were, and they looked thin and hungry. They also looked terrified.

"May we please sleep in your barn?" the boy asked tentatively. "We're very tired. We won't cause any trouble."

The Mage's instincts kicked in. "Come on in," he said. "I think that we can do better than a barn."

The two young people edged into the house.

"Sit down at the table, you two. I expect you'd like a bite to eat," said the Boffin.

She got out a loaf of bread and cut a couple of slices from it. The girl stared at it and couldn't help licking her lips. The

Boffin got out some butter and ham and made a couple of sandwiches, which were demolished in next to no time, so she made some more.

"What are your names, and where are you from, my dears?" asked the Boffin.

The Mage made some cocoa and gave two steaming cups to the two young people.

"My name is Carl and her name is Lynn. We won't cause any trouble. We'll leave in the morning."

"Where are you from?" the Boffin asked again.

Carl looked at Lynn.

"Well, sort of over there," he said, gesturing.

The Boffin looked at the Mage, puzzled?

"How did you get here?"

"We sort of, erm, stepped."

"You're from a different space? Where, exactly?"

The boy gestured again. This time the Boffin caught the direction he meant. It was different to the directions that the Mage and the Boffin usually stepped.

"Hm, we've never stepped in that direction. I didn't even know it existed," said the Boffin. She made a quick note to herself on her computer. "That's probably why we couldn't figure out where the disturbance was coming from."

"You know about stepping? Disturbance? Are you a witch? Are you a spy for the High Witch?" asked the girl.

The two young people looked like they might make a run for it.

"No, no, we don't even know this 'High Witch'," said the Mage. "Are you running away from her or something? You are safe with us. I am an expert in magic and my wife is a scientist of some repute."

"A scientist?" The boy and girl looked at the Boffin in amazement and fear. "You're not going to experiment on us are you?"

"Good heavens, no. Is that what you think scientists do? Experiment on people?" asked the Boffin.

"Yes, cut them up. Force poisons down their throats. And laugh while they do it," said Lynn.

The Boffin was shocked and speechless.

"Who told you that scientists do that?" asked the Mage. "I promise you that my wife will do none of those things!"

He was almost laughing, but the young people seemed serious.

"Why, everyone knows that," said Carl. He hesitated. "Is it not true? There are no scientists any more where we come from."

"No, it's not true. Scientists are simply seekers after truth. Much like magicians. They just use a different approach. They certainly wouldn't experiment on people like you describe!"

The Boffin recovered herself. "So, you appear to be fugitives. Are you running from the High Witch? If so, why does she want you?"

"We don't know. Some of the High Witch's soldiers came to Lynn's house. Her grandfather, the one who taught us to step, told us to go, to step away. He said that he'd hold them off. I think he's dead."

Carl broke off to comfort Lynn.

"Poor kids," said the Mage. "You're not brother and sister then? What about your parents?"

"No, we aren't brother and sister. I don't remember my parents. Lynn's parents disappeared years ago. I was assigned to Lynn's house by the High Witch's men when I was small, almost a baby. We grew up together. I don't remember anywhere else."

The Boffin looked at the Mage and tilted her head towards the pair. He nodded and said to the pair "Please give me your hands a moment."

The two extended their hands and the Mage took them, only to jerk like he was stung.

"Ow! You have powerful protection. Is that your own? Let's try again."

He extended his hands to the two young people again. This time he held their hands for a minute or two before letting go.

"Thank you for letting me in. You are two powerful people. My guess is that the High Witch has somehow discovered that you might be a threat to her. Is that what happened?"

"We're powerful?" Carl looked at Lynn again. "Are we? No one ever told us that. It can't be true."

The Mage tossed a ball of fire at Lynn, who swatted it away with a gesture. It bounced off a wall and fell behind the sofa and the Mage hurriedly put it out.

"Do you know how did you did that, Lynn?" asked the Boffin, laughing.

"I don't know. I don't know how I did it. I just did it. Did I do something wrong?"

She was almost in tears.

"No, dear," said the Boffin. "My darling husband was just proving to you that you do have powers, and singed the carpet in the process. Can I hold your hands?"

The Boffin felt a strong protection force as she joined hands with the two. No wonder the Mage had jumped. She pushed past the protection which let her through and felt the two strong young minds behind it. She looked at the protection and decided that the two young people were the source. She looked at their minds and saw that they had a very strong bond. The power that they had was shared, and came from both sides, magical and scientific.

"Wow. Complex and strange. Thank you for letting us in. I don't think that either of us could have got in if you hadn't let us."

"Look," said Lynn.

She was holding a ball of fire much like the one that the Mage had tossed at her. She tossed it at Carl who caught it and looked at it. Then he tossed it back and created one of his own. Then they tossed the two balls of fire backwards and forwards between them, laughing. Finally, Carl squeezed the two balls out of existence.

"Wow," said Lynn. "What else can we do?"

The two young people were no longer scared and looked much more confident.

"Hmm, just a minute," said the Boffin.

She left the room and returned with one of her devices from her laboratory.

"This is broken," she said. "I know what needs to be done to it to fix it. How about you two take a look at it?"

The two young people looked at it.

"I'll have to open it," said Carl.

The Boffin indicated that they should go ahead. Carl twisted the case and it fell apart into two pieces.

Lynn and Carl studied it. Lynn looked up.

"Do you have any..."

The Boffin slid some wire and some tools across to them. Carl ignored the tools and cut some wire with little bursts of fire and fixed it in place inside the device.

Lynn twisted the device back together and pressed the button on it. The dial lit up but nothing else happened. She twisted the device apart again, and the two of them peered at it again.

"That one?" she asked Carl, pointing at a component.

"That's my guess. Do you have..."

The Boffin slid a component across the table. Lynn unfixed a component with one of the Boffin's tools and fitted the new component in its place. She closed the case and this time the dial lit up and showed some numbers and directions.

"How did we do that?" asked Carl. "I've never seen one of those before! What is it?"

"It's just a power meter. You used intuition, which is a skill on the magical side of the scale to fix an instrument which belongs to the physics side of the scale. That's quite unusual, though not unknown. You two have both magical and scientific talents in equal measure. Oh, by the way, we prefer to use the tools. To use magic for simple physical repairs, like you fixed the wiring, Carl, is showing off a bit. Though to be fair, I've done it myself when I can't find the tool."

Carl nodded.

The Boffin said "Tell us some more about the High Witch. Does she often send her men out to bring people in? I guess that if she just asked, people would make themselves scarce."

Carl thought a bit. "She sends out her men to arrest people, and they are never seen again. That's what happened to Lynn's parents. Gramps said that they didn't take us because we were so small. Some people say that she drinks blood, but I think that's just a story. Anyway, everyone obeys her. They're scared of her."

"But you got away."

"Yes, Gramps suddenly got up and told us to hold hands. Then he said 'Step out of here, my loves. Remember me and remember your Mum and Dad. Now, step!'. So we did, and we were in this space. We wandered around for a few days and ended up on your doorstep. Lynn said 'This place feels good. Let's knock on the door.'. So we did."

"You think it was the High Witch's men? What happened to your Gramps?"

Carl reflected. "Yes, I heard the Witch's men outside the door. As we were stepping Gramps collapsed, though I didn't see why."

"How would you like to stay with us for a couple of days? It should be safe enough."

Carl looked at Lynn. "But we seem to bring trouble down on everyone we meet."

Lynn looked into the far distance. "Yes, we should be safe here for a day or two. Are you sure?"

"Of course, dear. Now, how would you like a bath?" asked the Boffin.

She took them off one by one and showed them the bathroom. They weren't too happy about being separated, but loved the Boffin's state-of-the-art bathroom. The Boffin laid them out clothes which her own kids had used, and they returned looking much less like a pair of waifs and strays. Lynn's hair had a coppery sheen while Carl's hair was very fair, almost white.

The four of them passed the evening playing board games and generally chatting about the differences between the kids' space and their own space. Carl and Lynn were amazed to learn that the ruler was a normal person, with no special powers.

"How does he make people do what he wants, if he has no powers?" asked Carl.

"Why, he asks them nicely," said the Boffin, "and because he is King, they usually do it."

"But what if they don't want to do it?"

"Well, there's usually a reason. So they tell the King the reason, and then they negotiate a compromise. A good King only asks people to do things that they won't mind doing, though sometimes the King has to convince them. Or vice versa."

She thought a bit. "It's like your Gramps telling you to go to bed. He has no special powers, but you do it anyway. Or you discuss with him why you should be allowed to stay up longer."

When the young people were in bed, the Boffin threw up her readings onto the wall of the room. The Mage came and circled her waist with his arms from behind.

"Is this the latest readings?" he asked. "It looks pretty much OK. All green. But you aren't happy."

"Yes, it's all green at the moment. I've wrapped that camouflage charm of yours around the house, just to be safe, though. It'll look like we are the only ones here."

"That'll not fool anyone with real powers though."

She nodded. "Yes, and look what happens if I project it a week out."

She gestured and the numbers changed and then suddenly the colours changed to red.

"Hmm, not nice," said the Mage.

She turned in his arms and hugged him.

"I'm not going to back away from a fight," she said. "I'll not abandon those kids to whatever fate awaits them. I just can't."

"Neither can I. You know I won't. We've got a few days, and they are quick learners. The trouble is, we don't know what the threat actually is. We know it's almost certainly caused by the High Witch."

She kissed him. "It's funny isn't it. The more we study, the more we know. But we didn't even suspect that we could step in that direction. We've got things working pretty well in our own human space here. But now we seem to be attracting couples like Carl and Lynn. Remember Kitty and Terry and how we helped them? Maybe our roles have changed slightly, and our job now is to help these young couples, the powerful people from distant spaces, find their feet?"

"Maybe. I wouldn't mind that too much. I'm never bored, and it would be interesting. Anyway, let's go to bed."

In the morning the Boffin explained what they were going to do. "We are going to teach you as much as we can in the next week or so, but it's going to be hard. There's a crisis coming in about a week's time, and we'll do our best to help you get through it."

"Maybe we should just go," said Lynn. "We don't want to drag you into it."

The Mage shook his head. "It's coming anyway, whether you go or stay. I checked my oracle. We just have to get through it, and the best way is to make you two as strong as possible. Do you understand how important and powerful you are?"

"Us? No, we're not grown-ups. We're not important. We're not powerful."

"Stop that!" snapped the Boffin. "You need to believe in yourselves. It's critical."

She grabbed the two of them in a containment field and made them immobile. Carl went red in the face with effort and his hand crept slowly towards Lynn's, as hers did towards his. When they touched, the field collapsed. Carl and Lynn both gasped for air.

"We did it!" she said. "

"Pretty good, but you need to be better."

This time the Boffin separated them before she sent up the containment field. Lynn and Carl struggled hard but couldn't break the field.

"We can't do it! Oh no," wailed Lynn.

"Yes, we can," said Carl. "We just need to work together. We don't actually need to touch!"

"Oh, of course," said Lynn, and the field collapsed.

The Boffin considered. "That wasn't bad. Pretty good, actually," she said. "Now the Mage and I can work separately, but it seems that you two **have** to work together. You're different in that respect. Let's take a break now."

They worked with the kids, sometimes alone and sometimes together. Lynn and Carl were learning really fast and sometimes the Boffin and the Mage had to extend themselves a little, which they considered to be a positive. But the Boffin knew that they were nowhere near as strong as the High Witch was going to be.

On the fifth day, the Mage declared a holiday, so they stepped to the dragon space. Immediately the Boffin knew that something was wrong. Something was bobbing in the waves, and she ran down to see what it was. It was the corpse of a dragon. She spun around. The little shack was in ruins. Their belongings were scattered around the beach and the vines that draped the shack were dead and faded.

"Ahhhhhhhhhh!" she screamed and lightning flashed from her raised arms into the sky. Then she cried.

"Logic, dear, logic," said the Mage, who was grey and shaking. "Emotion is not going to serve us well, here. Logic."

"Oh, my dear, you must feel it worse than me. I'm so sorry. I must concentrate!"

But she fired off another bolt into the heavens first. Just to stop her hands shaking.

The Mage stepped forward and a ball of lightning hit the dragon's corpse and it disappeared. He turned and gestured and the shack became whole. Their possessions lifted from the ground and disappeared into the shack. Another gesture and the dead vines disappeared. It was a grandiose use of magic, but he didn't care.

"We'll let the vines grow back naturally," he said. "I've put a protection spell around it, which we should have done before. Well, now we know that the High Witch is actively looking for you two. She must have detected our connection with you and searched for us because she couldn't see you. How petty she was, to destroy our lovely shack!"

"We're so sorry," said Lynn. "We had no idea that she would be able to trace us. We're sorry she destroyed your shack."

"Don't worry, dear. That can be fixed, but I feel angry about the poor dragon. I'm sure that we would have met up with the High Witch, sooner or later."

"I agree," said the Boffin. "Right, logic. We should take the fight to her before she does any more damage. Oh, our cottage! Let's get back, quick."

They stepped back worriedly, but everything was fine. The Boffin threw her latest readings on the wall.

"Well, there's you two, Lynn and Carl." She pointed to a blue patch with numbers which rapidly fluctuated. "The program doesn't know quite what to make of you. I can fix that later. Then there's this blue patch which seems to be getting closer. It's not the Witch, it's not bright enough. I think that we are about to get a knock on the door. Stay here, you two."

She went to it and opened it. Two large men stood there, one with his fist raised to knock on the door.

"Hullo ma'am, I'm Smith and this is Jones. We are looking for two fugitives, and we believe that they are here."

"Was it you two who killed the dragon and wrecked our shack?" asked the Boffin with a tinge of steel in her voice.

"No, ma'am. That was a bad business. Some youngsters given weapons that they shouldn't have been trusted with. We would not do that. We are professionals."

"Suppose that I told you that the 'fugitives' were not here?"

"Sorry, ma'am, I would not be able to believe you. Our information is correct, I believe."

"Suppose the two 'fugitives' were here, and we refused to give them up. What would you do?"

"Well, ma'am, we would have to report back, and no doubt further action would be taken. Not by us, I might add."

He managed to give her the impression that the whole thing was distasteful to him.

"You'd better come in. Please note that we have defences in place."

"Thank you, ma'am," said Jones. "We understand. We don't intend to cause any trouble, I assure you."

The Boffin led the way to their kitchen where the others were waiting.

"This is Smith and that is Jones, everyone. They are looking for two fugitives, they say. Dear, can you make them a cup of tea. Please sit down, gentlemen. Biscuit?"

"Thank you, ma'am and sir. That's very kind of you."

"So, what exactly is your mission, gentlemen?"

"We are to locate and return two fugitives who have escaped from our ruler, the High Witch. We have been given this location as the place where we can find the fugitives, and this device to get us here and back."

He showed the Boffin the device. Neither he nor Jones acknowledged the presence the two young people. They were without doubt professionals.

"So the Witch had nothing to do with the dragon and our shack?" asked the Mage.

"No sir, not directly. It was just some idiot kids she'd sent to look for the fugitives. Just so you know, sir, the dragons appeared over the city and smashed a few things, made a few holes in roadways and bridges and disappeared. No casualties, except someone who fell into a hole. The High Witch couldn't touch them, though she put on quite a firework display."

He nodded his approval of the dragons' actions.

"You don't seem to like her much, gents."

"She's our employer, sir. We can't have an opinion about her."

The Boffin and the Mage glanced at each other. They liked Smith and Jones.

"Well, Smith and Jones, suppose we were to agree to you taking the two fugitives back, but only if you took us, too, would you have any objection to that?"

"You don't have to do that!" said Carl.

"We do," said the Boffin. "It still annoys me that she sent the people who killed the dragon and wrecked our shack!"

Smith looked at Jones. "That's OK by us, sir. We have no orders to the contrary."

"We are all agreed, then?" The Boffin looked around at the Mage and the two young people.

"Then let's do it."

Smith and Jones stood up. "Please hold hands," said Jones. His partner took out his device and Jones held his wrist. They all joined hands in a circle and Smith pressed a button on the device and suddenly they were standing in the courtyard of a castle.

The Mage looked around and sniffed. "Too ornamental. A castle should be functional."

"This way, please," said Smith, and the two big men directed them into the castle.

As they walked through the corridors to meet the High Witch, the Boffin looked around.

"I see what you mean, dear. I mean to say! Suits of armour every five metres. Crossed swords and shields on every wall between them. Huge tapestries. Arched doorways, leaded windows. It's a bit much," she said.

The throne room was an immense room with a vaulted ceiling, with leaded glass windows high on the walls and behind the throne. As they walked towards the throne, the backlighting meant that they couldn't see who was on the throne.

Torches on the wall suddenly burst into flame, and curtains covered the windows behind the throne, and the High Witch was revealed. She appeared to be a young woman in her low thirties, and she was wearing a low cut green dress which clung tightly to her body. The Boffin immediately hated her even more than she had before.

"Hi, Your Witchiness. I understand that you are looking for our friends here," the Boffin said, deliberately trying to be offensive.

She gestured at Lynn and Carl.

"Thank you for returning them," said the High Witch, visibly controlling herself. "They were about to cause me a great deal of trouble."

"They were? Why is that? By the way, I said nothing about returning Lynn and Carl. They are under our protection."

"Yes, they were about to serve as a focus for forces opposed to me. My mirror warned me. I don't allow opposition."

She smiled. "So they are under your protection, are they? Whose protection are **you** under?"

The High Witch gestured and the Boffin could not move. The Witch laughed and the two young people marched like robots to stand beside her. The Boffin desperately struggled to free herself from the spell or field that was holding her immobile. She could imagine that the Mage was struggling similarly. Nothing seemed to work.

Suddenly she heard the Mage's voice in her head. "Don't struggle, my dear. Use your logic to find a solution, and I will try to use my gifts to find one too."

The High Witch looked at the Mage. "Hmm, you're cute. Come and join me."

The Mage's voice in her head said "Concentrate, my dear! Concentrate!"

222

To her horror the Boffin saw the Mage out of the corner of her eye move towards the High Witch. He was taking reluctant step after reluctant step towards her. His brow was sweating with the effort of resisting, but he was being forced to approach the High Witch.

She tried to shout to Lynn and Carl. She tried to form the word "together". The next thing she knew was the ground coming up to hit her in the face and the roar of the word being repeated at her.

"TOGETHER!!"

The Mage came to, lying on the floor just below the steps to the throne.

"What happened?" he asked. "Ouch, my head."

"The High Witch lost the fight. I'm not sure how, but the power came through me and Carl," said Lynn. Little sparks were still crackling from her fingers. There were singe marks at various places on the floor and the throne had lost an ornament from the top of the back.

The Mage gingerly climbed to his feet and ran over to where the Boffin was lying on the ground supported by Carl. She was bleeding heavily from her nose.

"I don't lige dis," she said thickly. "I dink my dose is brokerd."

The Mage ran his finger down her nose and the bleeding stopped. Her nose straightened but forever afterwards had a slight bend in it.

"Thanks, dear. What happened?" said the Boffin.

"Pain relief?"

"Just a little, please."

The Boffin looked around. Not much had changed apart from the marks of the battle, but the Witch was cowering on her throne. Her facade of youth had evaporated, and she looked closer to sixty or seventy.

"So much for using my powers of logic to figure out a solution. All I could think of was to stop her taking the Mage away from me. Then I was trying to tell Lynn and Carl to work together, and the floor hit me in the face," she said.

"We got your message," said Carl. "We were trying to work together but it wasn't making any difference. Then we sort of extended our reach and suddenly the power was flowing in, and we easily overcame the Witch. I don't understand it. You two fell over and knocked yourselves out when she let go of you."

"I think I know what happened," said the Boffin, tapping her pocket device. "Magic and Science work differently here from our home space. The power is spread over everyone. Back home and in most spaces, certain people, like us, have the power and channel it, and most people have little or none. Here, the power is not concentrated but certain people can channel it. You have to call on it, which you accidentally did. If we'd known, we could have trained you differently."

"How did the Witch get her powers then?" wondered Carl.

"The same way as you did. She drew on the power which is spread through everyone. The power of Magic and Science is not good or evil. It's how you use it. Boy, was she strong! But enough people must have had enough of her, so the Science and the Magic flowed to you and not her. We should never have faced her directly."

"I think that you are right. That's what happened, though we didn't know it at the time," said Carl. "We've still got some of the power that we called on."

"But what about the Witch? What do we do with her?" asked the Mage.

"The Witch can do nothing.," said Lynn. "She has no power now, and is unlikely to be able to gather any again. The mood of our space is against her."

The Boffin drew on the power of the space to check, and saw that it was as Lynn said. Working this way was strange, but strange in a nice way, and when she considered the space itself the word "friendly" came to mind. She doubted that it would have seemed like that ten minutes before.

Lynn walked over to the throne and the former High Witch flinched away.

"She doesn't even remember what happened. She's just scared. She doesn't remember being the High Witch. We'll find her a home somewhere where she can be looked after properly. The poor thing's mind is partly destroyed."

Lynn calmed the former Witch with her mind then she and Carl sent her off with Smith and Jones, with orders to find her a home. Smith and Jones could be trusted to do the right thing.

"What will you do now, you two?"

"Well first we'll bring back all the people that the Witch made disappear," said Carl. "The power of Magic and Science in this space didn't give her enough power to destroy them, it seems, so they are in a sort of limbo. Then we will have to start to work out how this space should be governed. We'll probably hold some elections eventually. Let the people of the space decide."

The Mage said "You are both still very young. I suggest that you get Smith and Jones to help you out at first."

Carl nodded, then thought a bit. "Oh, it seems that Gramps had a heart attack and the Witch's men took him to hospital.

We'll go over and see him later. Not all the Witch's men were infected by her spite, it seems."

"There's one thing that I must do before we go," said the Mage.

He gestured, but nothing happened.

"Gather the power first, dear," said the Boffin.

"Oh, yeah, of course. I forgot," he said, and gestured again.

Four youths in military uniforms appeared. They reacted in shock and surprise.

"You four killed a dragon and wrecked our shack. What do you have to say for yourselves?" asked the Mage.

"We thought that the dragon was attacking us, sir!" said one of them. "We used our weapons in our own defence, we thought. We only realised afterwards that it was just interested in us."

"Hmm," said the Mage.

He could see that they were telling the truth. A swooping dragon could look as if it was attacking, and that is what he saw in their minds. "But what about our shack? Why did you wreck that?"

"We're sorry, sir. The High Witch sent us to find the two fugitives, and we conducted a thorough search. But then things got out of hand, and we ended up wrecking it, sorry sir. It was stupid of us, sir."

Again the spokesman was telling the truth. The Mage thought that maybe some of the spite of the High Witch had spilled over into the boys. They didn't seem to be bad boys, and were definitely regretful.

"You're very lucky, lads. My wife was very angry when she saw the dragon and even angrier when she saw our shack."

The troopers looked at the Boffin and changed into wobbling jellies, figuratively speaking.

"We're truly sorry, sir. What is our sentence?"

"Sentence?" The Mage had not thought that he was judging them, but they obviously did.

"Well, I sentence you to four weeks community work. Make repairs on the roofs of a few poorer people. Dig some old folks' gardens for them. That sort of thing. You never know, you might get a taste for it."

"Thank you, sir. And ma'am. Thank you."

The Mage sent them back.

"Now, we will have to leave you, you two. Come and see us some time. We'd love to hear how you are getting on. Goodbye for now."

"Thank you for everything. I think things are going to change for the better," said Carl. "I feel it somehow."

The Mage shook their hands and the Boffin hugged them, then they stepped, waving goodbye, back to their own space.

"Well, that was interesting," said the Mage.

"Especially when she tried to draw you towards her. We really underestimated that space. Or rather, we overestimated our powers in a foreign space."

The Mage waved his hands and the Boffin looked exactly like the Witch had earlier.

"Stop it!" said the Boffin. She was not pleased. "Green doesn't suit me!"

The Mage realised his mistake and let her revert. He didn't often make serious mistakes in their relationship, but this time he knew that he had. "Sorry, it was meant as a joke. I can see now that it wasn't funny. Not funny at all."

The Boffin let him hold her. She wondered how long she could pretend to be still annoyed with him. She decided not to tease him as he looked so worried. She kissed him.

"It was horrible to be powerless," she said. "We waltzed in there, full of confidence, and then we could do nothing. We were over confident. Let's learn from that."

"You're right. We were over confident. But we did have a little power. I sorted your nose out. I resisted the Witch's pull to some extent."

"That's true. I managed to communicate with the kids, too. I'll have to figure out a way to store the power, in case we find ourselves in a place where we can't connect to the local source. A sort of battery, I guess. I think we are going to find ourselves in similar situations in the future."

"I think so too, my dear. It seems that our roles have changed to helping youngsters like Carl and Lynn through difficult situations. I feel, however, that while we may be less powerful in other spaces, the people that we will be helping will not be restricted in the same way, since they will be natives of the other spaces."

She leaned into him, and he enfolded her in his arms. "I trust your feelings, dear, and I agree with your reasons. But my blood ran cold when the Witch was drawing you towards her."

"Don't worry, my dear. You know that I will never leave you. While my body might have come to stand beside her, my heart would still have been with you. You know that."

And she did.

***

A Chat with God

The Mage and the Boffin were a long way from home. They'd been visiting some friends in a distant space and had stopped off on their way back to their home space. One of the Boffin's students would probably have said that they been visiting alternative Universes, if he or she had known that the Mage and the Boffin could step between spaces.

But anyway, in the space or world or Universe where the Mage and Boffin had stopped off, a big battle was underway. To the soldiers of both sides, they were invisible. When they had first arrived, they were protected from harm, of course, but both sides could see them, and both sides naturally targeted them. So the Mage had hidden them both from view.

The Boffin plucked a bullet from the air and inspected it. "Hm, it's just a dumb projectile, a lump of metal. At least it's not an exploding bullet or a 'smart' bullet. The technology is pretty basic, then."

"Still deadly," commented the Mage. "I wonder what they are fighting about?"

A large shell landed nearby and dirt splattered against their protection.

"They're fighting about me, I expect," said a voice. "It's usually about me."

The Mage and Boffin turned. An oldish looking man with white hair and beard and long flowing robes was standing next them. He didn't seem happy.

"Hullo," said the Boffin. "Why would they be fighting about you?"

The old man looked to the west and then to the east. "Yes, they are fighting about me, or rather, about something they believe about me."

He turned to the Mage and the Boffin. "You're not from around here, are you? I figured as much when the bullets bounced off you or avoided you. I'm God, by the way."

"You're God?" said the Mage incredulously.

"Of this space, anyway." He paused thoughtfully. "Hmm, you call it a 'space', I see. Yes, I'm God. The people in this space are believers, and their belief has caused me to exist. I can see that you don't do things that way at home."

"Yes," said the Boffin. "We, well, our people, are either more or less interested in science or more or less interested in magic. We don't have a strong religion, but we do have some believers."

"You're lucky," said God. "I actually don't think that I existed before enough people believed strongly in me, but once I existed, I had always existed, it seems. You two are real people, so you don't have that existential problem."

"So what are they fighting about?"

"Apparently, according to their beliefs," he said gesturing to the east, "I said something about the way they worship me."

He gestured to the west. "They, on the other hand, believe something else."

"Did you say anything about the way that people worship you?

God snorted. "I said nothing about worship. Nothing at all. I didn't want them to worship me. I did once ask them to respect me."

"What did you want from them? I mean, after you started to exist."

"Once I existed, I existed for ever. I was by myself, and well, being anthropomorphic, I got lonely and wanted people around me, so I created the big explosion that created this Universe. You call it this 'space', of course. Good name. It didn't work out too well. I'm infinitely patient of course, so I didn't mind the billions of years it took to create all the matter, and for it to condense into stars, and for life to evolve on this small planet."

"From your face, that's when the trouble started," guessed the Mage.

"Yes, to create humans, I needed life to appear and for evolution to occur. That was tricky to get started but once it was going it only took a few billion years. The problem was that evolution happens because of competition. All life is founded on competition."

"Ah, so humans evolved to be competitive," said the Mage.

"Yes, and they insist on killing each other. Sad, isn't it?"

"It's much the same in our space," said the Mage, "but I don't think that we are nearly as aggressive as your people."

God nodded. "Yes, I think that is because they invented religion. They invented ME."

"But you're God. Couldn't you do something?"

God nodded again. "What do you do when humans start to wage a war in your space?"

"Well, we generally don't interfere. If we do, it usually makes things worse. Oh, I see!"

"Exactly. I tried many times to stop the wars, and every time I made things worse. One time I took one of them aside and said to him 'Look, I don't like all this killing. Please tell everyone to stop it.' He said 'Lord, I'll carve it on some stones and then everyone can see your commands and act on them.' I said 'Don't bother, here they are.' He went down the mountain with the stones, very happy with himself."

"What went wrong?"

"Well, a couple of things. I'd added a couple of other instructions, things about loving your mother and father, and not desiring your neighbours smart house and car and that sort of thing and one about listening to me, rather than all the false gods that were around at the time. Things that I thought would be useful to remember. I'd written the commands in the language and the idiom that they used at the time. But I should have kept it simple. Just a ban on all the killing. It just confused them."

"What else went wrong?"

"Well, I'll go into that, but shall we get away from all this killing?"

God waved his hand, and they were standing on the front porch of a pleasant house with a view over fields and meadows, down to a wide meandering river.

"Please sit down. I'll make some tea." God pottered off. He was back in a minute or two with a tray, with teapot, cups and two plates of biscuits.

"You know, for some reason, no one thought of a possible Mrs God," he said. "So, unless I actually manifest myself to a human, I'm always alone." He sighed.

"So what happened about the stones?" asked the Boffin, dipping her biscuit in her tea.

"Well, the chap I chose decided that having the stones meant that his people were 'chosen by God', and that meant that everyone else was not chosen and could be killed. In fact, he and others reasoned, it was his duty to kill anyone who was not one of his people. This was reinforced by another command, which was to have no other gods but me. I'd actually meant that they should not listen to the prophets of other gods, but I couldn't phrase it that way in the language that they used. So the killing went on."

"That must have been discouraging," commented the Boffin.

"Yes, it was. I was so discouraged that at one time I created a flood and drowned them all. That was tricky as some lived up mountains and I didn't want to completely flood everywhere, and also I had to preserve all the animals and plants. The animals hadn't caused the wars, of course. And the idea of killing everyone to stop them killing themselves was not exactly logical either, was it? I think I was a little crazy at the time."

"But there are people now, so did you recreate them?"

"No, I foolishly picked one man who I thought was better than all the rest, and told him to build a boat to save himself and his family. He floated around for a while, then ended up on a mountain. The floods drained away and I put all the animals and plants back. You wouldn't believe the silly stories that this incident gave rise to! In one, all the animals were carried in the boat, with the humans! As if that were possible. But it wasn't long before the killing resumed."

"This is a nice place you have here, God," said the Boffin. She was trying to stop God from becoming too depressed.

"Thank you. I spend a lot of time here, but it is lonely. Do you not have wars back in your space, Boffin?"

"Well, yes. For that matter, I don't think that we've seen a human space that doesn't have war. Humans seem to like them. You could be right that it stems from evolution and that competitiveness is built in to humans."

"Do you not have conflict between science and magic? It seems to me that having both science and magic in a space would lead to fighting."

"We do have competition, it's true, and we did have one huge war between science and magic, but that ended when one man absorbed all the power of science and magic into himself by accident and ended the war. He then passed the focus of science to me and the focus of magic to the Mage. We were both sympathetic to the other's field of expertise already, and we fell in love and were married. After that, there was still competition, but it is mostly just a friendly rivalry."

God nodded. "I wish something like that had happened in this space. I notice, though, that you both have traits from the other's field. You, my dear Boffin, are a mother figure, I think, and that leans to the magic side. The Mage is a father figure, and that leans to the science side."

The Boffin was startled. "Well, I never though of it that way," she said. "It could be true."

She looked at the Mage. "What do you think, dear?"

"Well, God may be right. We've never worried too much about keeping the roles and the foci separate. We often borrow techniques from each other and respect each other's field, and the crossover in our traits that God mentioned probably helps."

"Anyway, God, I suppose that you tried again, to stop people killing one another?"

"Oh yes, several times. Many times! I had some success when I manifested myself, and taught a group of people to love one another and restrain their natural aggression."

God took on the appearance of a younger man. "But I'd upset the authorities, and they killed me rather gruesomely, or rather they killed the body that I had at the time. Even for me it was difficult to come back from that and it took a few days until I was able to return. This shocked and horrified my followers, so I had to leave them. The stories that resulted from that were strange. People rationalised what they saw, and fitted it into their view of the world."

He paused. "Well, the movement took off, and became a religion which spread widely. It did seem to tone down the killing and the wars just a bit. People did consider the feelings of other people more. I was quite pleased, at first, but the wars started again soon enough."

The Mage said "When we were just starting out we tried to stop all the wars. On one occasion we took all the Kings and Queens and put them in a space where they could harm no one, and told them to make peace. Eventually they did, but when we sent them back, one King treacherously attacked and took over all the other kingdoms. We managed to stop him after a while, but we learned a valuable lesson from that. We only try to influence things and interfere directly as little as possible."

God laughed. "Well, maybe I'm a slow learner. I've tried again a few times since but it always ended badly. But lately, like you, I've just been a spectator."

"So, what were those two armies fighting about?"

"Well, both sides believe in me, and both are offshoots of the religion I talked about before. One lot believe that their leader is an avatar of me, and that everything he says is the literal truth. It's not true of course. The other lot don't believe in this doctrine of infallibility, and they loathe the rituals that their enemies love. So they are trying to persuade each other with bullets and bombs! Madness!"

The Mage asked "Are you not interfering in this war, then?"

God snorted. "No, I've not interfered for a thousand or so years. I feel so sorry for those who suffer through these wars, though, that I've a space that I send them to, where everything is idyllic. It makes me feel a little better."

"You don't think that you need a bit of balance do you, God? What about the environment? What part of you worries about that? Is there a part of you that encompasses the mother figure?" asked the Mage.

"The environment? I'm always trying to persuade them to save some species or another! As for the 'mother figure' thing, maybe you are right, and maybe I do need some balance. Over the millennia and the millions of years I've thought about that, and meeting you two I can see that there are advantages. A shared burden. Someone to talk to. A different point of view."

"Then there're the kids," said the Mage.

"Kids!" said God. "Oh, yes, the kids!" He was lost in his own thoughts for a while.

"Well," said the Mage, "I would say that you possibly do need balance. Your approach is definitely paternal, as is mine, and there seems to be little corresponding maternal influence, like the Boffin provides in our space. It may improve things to have that influence. Most spaces that we have visited have a maternal and a paternal influence, or an equivalent. In some spaces, the males look after the offspring and the females do the providing, but the balance is there."

"Was there never any maternal influence in this space?" asked the Boffin.

God cast his mind back. "Well in the early days, there was a mother Goddess, but as rational thinking replaced mysticism she sort of faded away. My followers have always been aggressive, as you saw on that battlefield, and, they claim, favour a rational approach, which may have contributed to her eclipse. I wonder what happened to her? I've always been suspicious of magic and superstition, but you, my dear Boffin are able to accept it alongside your science? Maybe I'm wrong."

The Boffin replied "Of course. It helps to remember that you use intuition all the time. You expect the sun to come up every morning, and you are always right. Oh, you can justify your intuition by wrapping science around it and talk about the rotation of the earth and stuff like that, but inevitably, eventually, those equations will be inadequate and the sun will not rise. But until that day, your intuition will prove to be correct. You don't even think about it. Long before science existed people expected the sun to rise every morning, and it did! Your intuition is magical, not scientific."

She looked at her husband and smiled. "Besides, magic works, doesn't it, my love?" she said.

She kissed her hand and blew. A brilliant ball of light flew through the air to the Mage and touched his lips. He caught the ball of light on his hand, blew it and the ball of light flew back to the Boffin.

God mused a bit. "But surely there is science behind that phenomenon?" he asked.

"Sure," said the Boffin, "but it is still magical, isn't it?"

The Mage and the Boffin bade God goodbye and strolled down his drive. It would be rude to vanish right off his doorstep.

As they reached the road a woman turned into the gateway. An attractive woman, thought the Boffin. She was slightly more curvy than the Boffin's slim build, and her skin gleamed darker than the Boffin's fairly dark skin. She wore a colourful wrap around dress that caused the Boffin to break one of God's commandments, the one about coveting, and her long, dark, curly hair was studded with small white flowers. She had bracelets on her wrists and anklets around her ankles. Her feet were bare. Around her neck was a necklace supporting a single large pearl. She smiled and her smile lit up the space, or the world, or the Universe. The Boffin instantly liked her.

"Is he is in?" asked the woman.

The Boffin stepped forward and hugged her. "Yes, he's in. And I think he's ready."

"It's about time," laughed the woman. "It's been thousands of years. Millions. Thank you."

"For what?" asked the Mage. "Oh, you think we helped by being a couple?"

"Don't mind him, he can be a bit slow at times," said the Boffin.

The woman laughed and started off up the drive. She swayed in a way that the Boffin wished she could copy.

"Good luck," called the Boffin.

"Thank you," responded the woman.

The Mage swept the Boffin into his arms and kissed her thoroughly. She linked her fingers behind his neck.

"You don't have to prove anything, my love," she said. "She's a very attractive woman, the Goddess, but I know my man. It's nice of you, though. Now let's go home."

The Mage laughed. "It wasn't that. It was the thought of millennia without you, my dear. But it's nice of you, though!" he said teasingly.

He kissed her again, then slipped his arm around her waist, and she did the same, and they took the step that took them home.

***

Epilogue - Reflections

"Ah yes," said the Mage. "I remember those days. Fun times, mostly! Remember the early days, when we were helping Simon establish his reign? We didn't know what we were doing half the time!"

"Yes, but we were able to reliably tell whether people were sincere or had ulterior motives, and that helped. Most people had good intentions, though, didn't they? The war had shaken everyone up, and everyone wanted things to get better."

"We've seen many different spaces, haven't we? But we keep coming back to home, and to dragon space. Those are the two that we spend most time in."

"Yes, and we've made a few spaces of our own over the years," the Boffin said. "We spent a lot of time in the early days in our own 'safe space', do you remember?"

"I do! That was before we became more confident, and found our cottage and settled there, of course. There were no people in our safe space, and it was lonely."

"Yes," she said, "But there's something odd about the stories. Some of them seem slightly different from what I remember. Just small details, nothing major."

The Mage paused for thought. "Maybe they are stories from spaces near to the spaces that we remember, that we have lived in. Or maybe the stories have simply been passed from person to person and details have been accidentally changed. Remember the king who started off the line of kings and queens who change into a dragons when they get older? I remember his daughter as a young blonde girl, and his son as fair-haired too. In the story they are dark skinned, with dark hair. But does it matter?"

240

"Not really, I suppose. So long as the story is told. Maybe a Mage and a Boffin exist who remember the stories that way."

The Mage nodded reflectively. They sat quietly for a while. She drank her tea, and the Mage drank an infusion of a coffee-like bean from a distant space.

"I notice that Smith and Jones figure in a couple of the stories, and that's strange," said the Boffin, eventually. "There's nothing special about them, no magic and no science. They've no powers, and I don't think that they live enormously long lives, but they turn up in the stories, and I remember them being around in other adventures of ours, too."

"Oh, they are special, my dear, but not in the way that we are. Sometimes they are policemen, sometimes they are security men. Often they are military people. They are close to the focus of power in some spaces and stories. They represent 'integrity' and 'stability', I think. Sometimes 'peace keeping', or an 'arm of authority'."

"Maybe they should have their own book of stories, dear. Maybe we would be minor players in some of their stories. That would be nice."

He nodded. "What do you think of our stories, though?"

"Every single one of them reminds me of other adventures of ours! There are so many stories that could be told. Will more of them be told, do you think?"

"I think so. I think that someone will tell our stories, even if it is not this author. Even if we are called by different names. But this author does intend to write more of our stories so you can look forward to that, at least."

"Oh I will. I will. Will other people enjoy these stories too, do you think? After all, they are so interesting to us because they are about us."

"I hope so, my dear. I hope so."

***

Endnote

All the Mage and the Boffin stories so far written are available in eBook format as a single book. You can find it at most eBook publishers.

Unfortunately when I came to make the eBook into a paperback it came out too long, so I split the paperback into two volumes. They can be found at Amazon.

There is a distinct possibility that I might write more Mage and Boffin stories so keep a look out for further eBooks and paperbacks in the series.

www.ingramcontent.com/pod-product-compliance
Lightning Source LLC
Chambersburg PA
CBHW021029130626
46552CB00005B/1747